Copper Kettle

Books by Frederick Ramsay

The Ike Schwartz Mysteries
Artscape
Secrets
Buffalo Mountain
Stranger Room
Choker
The Eye of the Virgin
Rogue
Scone Island
Drowning Barbie
The Vulture
Copper Kettle

The Botswana Mysteries
Predators
Reapers
Danger Woman

The Jerusalem Mysteries
Judas
The Eighth Veil
Holy Smoke
The Wolf and the Lamb

Other Novels
Impulse

Copper Kettle

An Ike Schwartz Mystery

Frederick Ramsay

Poisoned Pen Press

First Edition 2017

10 9 8 7 6 5 4 3 2 1

Library of Congress Catalog Card Number: 2016952021

ISBN: 9781464207822 Hardcover
9781464207846 Trade Paperback

Poisoned Pen Press
6962 E. First Ave., Ste. 103
Scottsdale, AZ 85251
www.poisonedpenpress.com
info@poisonedpenpress.com

Printed in the United States of America

To Jeff Ruby and Andy Garman,
whose perception and vision
led them where three Episcopal
and one Lutheran Bishop would not go.
Many thanks and God bless.

Acknowledgments

To The Evil Editor Barbara, and Robert, and all the gremlins who work at Poisoned Pen Press, who turn stories into books for those of us who dream them up, thank you.

Foreword

First: a caveat. The names, places, and events described in this book are purely fictional. There is, in fact, a Buffalo Mountain in Floyd County Virginia. There is a town named Floyd which is the county seat. They do exist. Buffalo Mountain is beautiful, the town charming. You can Google the mountain and take a virtual hike to its summit. The view from there, they say, is unequaled anywhere. Speaking as a resident of Arizona and a visitor to the Grand Canyon, I might argue the point. At any rate, on a clear day, they say, one can see all the way to North Carolina to the south and some claim west to Tennessee as well. The mountain is now a state park and the domiciles that remain that once housed its population of sturdy mountain folk are vacation rentals, complete with running water, kitchens and so on. The people who grew up, raised families, and died there are, for the most part, scattered across the country and their stories relegated to history. In any event, neither they nor their lives form any part of what you will read here.

For an authentic peek at life on the mountain during this time period, read Richard C. Davids, *The Man Who Moved a Mountain,* a portion of which I quote here:

> *Walled in by surrounding hills, the people of the Buffalo lived in a land of Brigadoon, captive to the unchanging ways of generations past. Theirs was a heritage of proud independence—but also of poverty*

and ignorance, fear, and superstition, violence and sudden death. Tales of the dark deeds on the Buffalo spread through the mountains and beyond.

—Frederick Ramsay 2017

Copper Kettle

(As sung by Joan Baez)

Get you a copper kettle, get you a copper coil
Fill it with new made corn mash and never more you'll toil
You'll just lay there by the juniper while the moon is bright
Watch them jugs a-filling in the pale moonlight.

Build you a fire with hickory, hickory, ash and oak
Don't use no green or rotten wood, they'll get you by the smoke
You'll just lay there by the juniper while the moon is bright
Watch them jugs a-filling in the pale moonlight.

My granddaddy made whiskey, his granddaddy did too
We ain't paid no whiskey tax since 1792
You'll just lay there by the juniper while the moon is bright
Watch them jugs a-filling in the pale moonlight.

Chapter One

Solomon McAdoo stepped back; a deep vertical line bisected his forehead beginning where his eyebrows met in the middle. Tending the fire could be touchy business. He needed to get it just right or Big Tom would have himself a duck fit. Too hot and the hooch would be mostly water and the thump keg would fill up with mash. Too cool and you got nothing. The folks from the city who bought his whiskey were particular about what they paid for. Big Tom kept the best for them. The try hooch, the first drippings, he cut with water pretty good and put in mason jars and sold to the nigras for two bits. A jug would set them back six. They weren't in no position to complain and, anyway, it did what they wanted it to do—get them a Saturday night drunk, so there you go. Now the Lebruns, them that live on the other side of the mountain, they tried watering all of theirs down, figuring them city folks wouldn't know no better, and they ain't sold none since. Those Lebruns were always the ones to short the count in a cord so, what did you expect? Yep, if you get a name selling bad corn likker, you are in trouble and that's the truth. Never could trust the Lebruns. They say some of them might have lit out for Lynchburg or Baltimore where the pickings were easier for anyone disinclined to turn an honest dollar. Good riddance, if that were true.

The blue jays had been sounding their "jay, jay!" when he climbed the hill and ducked into this copse. A light breeze made the leaves dance. The silver maples turned their leaves over. Rain coming, for sure. By the time Solomon reached the still and contemplated what he had to do, the jays quit their squawking. Had they flown away figuring there wouldn't be any more mash spillage for them?

Across the creek, a limb broke free from an old oak with a sharp crack...Solomon began to shake. He sat on the ground and squeezed his eyes tight shut and hugged his knees. After a minute or two, the shaking stopped. He took a deep breath and stood and brushed the leaves from his mostly out-at-the-elbows Army jacket. The birds were chirping again. Birds were funny critters. Some folks say they can read your mind. How a little bitty bird might do that was a puzzle. Solomon stepped up to the still and slipped a few sticks of oak on the hearth. They flared and then burned easy and clean. No smoke meant no one would stumble on Big Tom's operation. The kettle rumbled on like nothing happened. He laid a hand on the thump keg, and then the big kettle. It seemed about the right amount of hot for each. He took a deep breath and exhaled. Grandpa would be okay with what he'd done. He thought he heard a footstep behind him.

The shotgun blast took off most of the back of his head. The report scattered the jays and startled the deer further down the creek. Solomon pitched forward. His fall knocked the kettle off its stone hearth. It fell on its side. The out-pipe separated from the kettle and the lid sailed off. The kettle itself rolled into the creek spilling its sweet mash. Like dominos, the thump keg and coil box followed. A day's worth of corn squeezings and most of the mash spilled into the creek and washed away.

• • ● • •

The shot echoed through the forest and caused Jesse Sutherlin to flinch and turn in the direction from which it seemed to have come. His brother, Abel, lifted an eyebrow.

"Somethin' wrong, Jesse?"

"No, it's nothing. I've been hearing gunshots in the woods my whole life. Probably just somebody hunting squirrels, though that sounded like a mighty big gun for squirrels. So, okay, nothing to be het up about." His brother didn't seem convinced. "See, it's just, I don't rightly know, Abel, but since the war, a gun going off when I ain't expecting it makes me start a bit. Like I need to know where and when, somehow."

"You and your old war. Seems like none of you all that went into that war come out like you was 'fore you joined up."

"You got a point there. It did change us some. Me, not so much, but you take Solomon. He's a proper mess. Anyway, over there, a shot didn't mean what it does here. In the trenches you want to know who's doing the shooting and why. If it was the Fritzies shooting and you were sitting in the forward trench, you know, you squared up and got your helmet on if you'd took it off earlier. It could mean they was coming, though usually we would have had mortar rounds and artillery first. Maybe you'd risk a peek through the parapet or use one of them periscopes to see. If it was one of our boys you could relax. He was probably just taking a pot shot at one of them just to keep them honest, like."

"Did you ever shoot one of them Germans?"

"You ask me that most every day. And I tell you the same thing every day, 'I can't say for certain.' See, mostly you just shoot at the place where they're at. Only the sharpshooters, the Limeys called them *snipers* for some reason, them fellers would try to pick off a particular target. The rest of us, hell we just aimed our Springfield in the general direction and squeezed the trigger, cocked and fired again as fast as we could. They called it 'laying down a field of fire.' I reckon they figured if enough bullets was in the air, one of them would soon or late hit someone. If you made into one of their trenches, there wouldn't be much shooting. Fighting there was with knives, bayonets, clubs, or anything handy, even a shovel maybe."

"All that shooting at what could be empty space seems kind of wasteful, don't it?"

"Boy, you ain't seen waste 'til you get yourself in the Army. Food, bullets, hell, even guns. You wouldn't believe what we left out on them battlefields. Germans, French, everybody did it.

War ain't tidy, Abel. Anyway, I suppose it is likely that one of them bullets which ended up in a German soldier might have come out of my gun, my rifle. They're particular about what you call your piece in the Army."

"So, how come you only check the direction of a gun going off, but Solomon like to have a conniption fit?"

"He's got what they call Shell Shock. Some of the fellers, mostly from the city, I think, just went to pieces out there. Shooting didn't come natural to them. All the mortar rounds coming in some days for maybe five hours without stop and then a big artillery shell would knock out twenty yards of trench with all the troops in it. It weren't a pretty sight and some of them just snapped. The officers and NCOs would try to talk them down, but from that day on, they were pretty much useless. Some they shipped home. Some just went plumb crazy. Solomon, well, he's got it bad. They sent him back to the field hospital for a bit, but after a week the docs sent him to the front again. They said he just needed a rest. They did that to a lot of tin hats who were afflicted that way, you could say. Well, he did seem some better, but then the shelling started up and he'd fall apart again. Me and a big strapping dairy farmer name of Spence who came from some place up there in Pennsylvania sort of took Solomon on and kept him upright. That way, he did make it all the way through the war and back home and that's saying something. You need to give him a wide berth, Abel. I don't want you ragging on him like them tow heads from over the other side of the mountain, the Eveleth brothers, and them other boys do. He can't help himself."

"Yeah, if you say so, but it's a hoot when they sneak up on Solomon and set off a firecracker or a scatter gun."

"Yeah, well, don't let me catch you doing anything like that, you hear?"

"If you say so, only I don't rightly see the harm in it."

"You would if you was Solomon."

Chapter Two

The forest floor with its ferns and this year's supply of new fallen leaves gave way to a wider, sunlit path and that led to a road. Not a paved road. Nothing in this part of the state had been paved, nor would it be for another fifteen years and not in the mountain for another two decades after that. Dirt in the spring, dust in the summer, mud in the fall and winter. You had to go all the way to the county seat if you wanted to see any paved roads that amounted to anything much. You could find evidence on some of the older ones in the area of the corrugated construction put there when timbering had been big, but that would be a while back. Most of the marketable timber had been cleared and the forests were mostly new growth, young oaks and quick-growing tulip poplars, and pine. The stately chestnut trees which had once sustained whole families and provided a lively business for more than a few in the past, had by now succumbed to the blight and had fallen, or soon would.

"So, you went over there as a private and come back an officer?"

"Yep. Things got so bad like we were losing officers right and left and so they figured 'We need to hang on to these West Point monkeys. Let's put a couple of the yokels up front instead. We can afford to kill off as many of them as is necessary. Ain't nobody going to miss them.' So, they made me an officer."

"It weren't like that. Come on, Jesse. How come you got them gold bars and Solomon got a little bitty stripe?"

"Well, it were like this, them officers thought they were fighting in Cuba or Chancellorsville or someplace like that. They'd stand there like they were old Stonewall himself and practically begged to be shot. I reckon it was because of our commander for a time, a one star general from up in New York someplace. We were all part of the Rainbow Division. Well, General Douglas McArthur would walk around out in the open and them Krauts would shoot away but, it was like he was bullet proof or something. He'd stroll along the trench mouth chatting up the boys who were scrunched down as low as we could get and he'd say things like, 'Evening boys, you getting fed good?' things like that. So, them Shavetails, seeing the general out there bold as brass, figured they had to be like their hero, only none of them led a charmed life like he done. He finally had to write out an order that said they should stop being foolish 'fore we was plumb out of second lieutenants."

"And that was why you was made a…what do you call them…a Shavetail? I don't believe that. That there medal with the cross on it that they pinned on you must have had something to do with it."

"Well, maybe you're right and maybe not. Anyway the platoon was shorthanded in the officer department and they figured as how I had the respect of the men, they'd put me in charge."

"You reckon I could be an officer?"

"Abel, don't wish for something too hard. You might get it to come true. The Army is no place for a boy with a future."

"Well, shoot. You think I got a future?"

"If you don't do something dopey, you do. You keep up with your schooling, get you a real job and most of all, get off this mountain."

Abel frowned at the last bit. He couldn't imagine living anywhere else but right here on Buffalo Mountain.

They walked along the path that led to the sawmill. Where it intersected the road, Jesse paused.

"This is where I leave you, brother."

"Jesse, are you sure about this? Did you talk to Ma at all?"

"Ain't nothing to talk about. We're strapped. Selling moonshine is against the law and 'fore you can say jack-be-nimble some federal man is going to come out here and bust up that still and maybe haul your grandpa off to the poky, Uncle Bob too. Maybe worse, allowing for how folks feel about revenue agents on the one hand and about their stills on 'tother, there could be some shooting. Make that there *will* be shooting. Then where will we be? No sir, I have seen all the gunplay I care to and ain't in a mood to fight with anybody no more."

"Well, if you say so, but working for Old Stick-in-the-Mud Anderson?"

"Why not? He pays a fair wage, twenty-five cents an hour, and after a year he's likely to bump it up a nickel. That will buy some good eating, Abel."

"I hear the railroad workers get a whole dollar, maybe a dollar and a half an hour. Twenty-five cents don't sound like much to me."

"Yeah, well the railroad doesn't run through here. I'd have to move over to Roanoke and, besides, they ain't hiring anyway. I asked."

"Still, I don't see why twenty-five—"

"Listen Abel. You listen good. I ain't got a skill, you understand? I ain't been to no proper school. I can do a little reading and figuring and that's it. I can scratch-farm some corn and 'taters. If I had decent bottom land, maybe make a living farming. But we don't have land like that and the only real schooling I ever got was from the U.S. Army. They taught me the only skill I can rightly claim—how to kill folks. Well, there ain't a big market for that anymore. I tell you, the dumbest thing I ever done was to turn down a chance to stay over there in Europe. They wanted volunteers to go fight the Russian communists, or anarchists, or whatever they was. I was an officer and they needed them, you know? So, I gave it some thought and then what did I do? I, like a ninny, turned it down. 'No, sir,' I said. 'The government said they would take care of us boys when we got back, yes sir. They was to be finding jobs as soon as we got back to home. It's 1919 and things is booming.' Nobody figured on a bust and President Wilson wasn't saying nothing. Rumor had it he is *non compos mentis*, which is the way them smart folks who been to college say he's out of his mind somehow. So, we come back and nobody has done anything. Everybody just wants to forget the war, the deaths, all of it. I tell you, Abel, if I hadn't been an officer, I would have had to walk home from Baltimore. I finagled me a train ticket to Roanoke and one for Solomon and here we are. We're back, near a year has gone by, and them that made the promises ain't done squat. So I will take what I can get, thank you very much."

"Grandpa says the men who drive out from Roanoke will pay two, sometimes three dollars a gallon for his good drinking whiskey. Two gallons a day, that there is four dollars and near twice what you'd get at the mill and you don't have to do no work. Just mix the mash, tend the fire, and find you a place to sit under a shade tree and wait. On a good week, Big Tom turns out 'bout ten or maybe even twelve gallons. That's way better money."

"Ten is a stretch, Abel. Twelve is a brag. Yep it's way better and riskier. Listen, I ain't thinking of stopping that enterprise. I just don't want to be in on it, see. Them Federal men have Colt six-shooters on their belts and that means they expect they might have to use them and are willing to 'cause the law is on their side. Any shooting back jumps the crime a mile. Well sir, like I say, I seen enough guns to last me a lifetime. I'm figuring on signing on at the sawmill and that's it."

Chapter Three

Jesse crossed the mill yard past men hauling lumber and trucks loaded with logs for sawing. The whine of the saw and the clap of new cut boards onto the carrier nearly drowned out anybody who might want to speak. Up close to the steam engines that drove the equipment, it even made thinking a chore. He tapped on the office building door and stepped in. The sour odor of new-sawn wood filled the air, even indoors. It was a smell one got used to when you worked as a sawyer and some said they missed it when they left for the day. Most folks didn't buy that, but agreed it was a whole lot pleasanter than slopping pigs or stirring mash.

Serena Barker with her starched shirtwaist and straw hat, presented a proper, one might say prim, presence behind a big oak desk inside the sawmill office. She had the benefit of a full nine years at the schoolhouse and had taught herself the intricacies of the Remington typewriting machine and single-entry bookkeeping. Because of that and because everyone agreed she was a "looker," she'd landed a job as a secretary/bookkeeper down at the mill. The pay wasn't as much as the mill hands', of course, but a dollar and a half a day seemed a pretty fair wage for a woman. After all, it was 1920 and the boom that the war brought had turned into a post-war bust. That, in its turn, had thrown a lot of men out of work so nobody was complaining, least of all Serena.

"Well, look at what the coon dog done dragged out of the tree," Serena said and gave Jesse a big, slightly crooked-toothed grin. "What brings the hero of Meuse-Argonne to Anderson's Mill? Not too many German soldiers hanging around here."

"How-do, Serena. It's a good thing there ain't. They like to scare me to death."

"I don't believe that, Jesse Sutherlin. What I hear is, they catch your name and scatter like chickens when a hawk flies by."

"All rumors. As to why I am here, they are saying up on the mountain that R.G. is hiring. I'm here to sign on."

"My, my, look at you. Farming not good enough for you?"

"Farming is just fine, Serena, but the land don't want to cooperate. A man will die of starvation on what that hillside produces in a year. They call it rock farming cause they're the only things that turn up in the field. Anyway I ate all the Jonny Ash Cake I care to. No, I need something steady."

"Hearth baking not your thing either? Well, you're right. Mister Anderson is hiring and he'd probably be happy to have you, but he isn't here right now. He had to run over to Roanoke for some supplies, he said. I think he just wanted an excuse to drive his new car."

"He bought a new car?"

"Yeah. Business is pretty good and he went and got himself a Piedmont Touring car. He went all the way to Lynchburg to get it. He drove it back the same day."

"Didn't he have an old Ford, a T model? What happened to that?"

"It's parked out back. He said he'd sell it to anyone with twenty-five dollars, cash money."

"That much for that broke down old flivver? It's eleven years old at least. Who'd want it and where's a man to find twenty-five dollars these days?"

"You work for him a week and a half and you do."

"And in the meantime I don't eat. No thank you."

"Whyn't you sit a spell and wait? He's been gone for a while. Unless he's got a whole lot of visiting to do, he should be back pretty soon."

"Well, thank you. I will do just that. So, how're you getting along now that you are a working woman?"

"I am just fine. I guess you are weary of talking about the war, but I have to ask, is it true the German soldiers eat babies?"

"Where'd you hear that? Lordy, they spread some pretty tall tales winding us up to go to war. Truth is I guess the Germans say the same kind of things about us. All meadow muffins, Serena. My experience with them fellows is they are just like us only they talk funny. Blood is just as red, put on their pants one leg at a time. Hell, sorry, my language turned a bit to the rough side in the Army. Anyway, we captured us a handful of them *soldaten* and one of them spoke a little American. You know something? He didn't have any more idea why he was at war than we did. We all had a laugh at that, I tell you."

"Really? I thought they was monsters and it was our patriotic duty to kill ever last one of them. They tried to get the Mexicans to come over the border, and all."

"Well, maybe. I didn't run into any Mexicans there or here, did you? No you didn't because, see, war is the business of rich old men in top hats up there in New York City getting fat on the profits they make selling stuff. You know, we found boxes of chemicals in a German redoubt that had U.S. of A. labels on them. We were told we wasn't to say nothing and they disappeared that night. But you know what I think? I think some Jasper up north was playing both sides and he's got American blood on his hands."

"That's awful. Is it true?"

"True as I'm sitting here admiring the rose among the thorns."

Serena blushed. "When did you decide to be a poet, Jesse Sutherlin?"

"The minute I laid eyes on you."

"Oh, you hush, now."

The door crashed open and a breathless Abel Sutherlin burst through. "Jesse, you got to come quick. Solomon's been shot dead. Sorry, hi there, Serena. Jesse, we got to go."

"Shot. When? How?"

"I don't know. Big Tom went up to his..." Abel looked at Serena. She smiled and nodded. "He went to the creek where he keeps his...tools—"

"You mean his still, don't you?" Serena said.

Yeah, yeah. How'd you...never mind. Anyway, Big Tom sent me down here to fetch you and say we should all get on up there to his place and figure out what to do."

"What to do? You get on Mister Anderson's telephone that's sitting right over there on Serena's desk and call the sheriff is what you do."

"I asked him that already. I asked if we should fetch the police. Grandpa says no. He says we can handle this our own selves like we always do."

"And 'like we always do' is a very bad idea. Serena, I am really sorry, but I got to run. Will you tell R.G. that I was here and if he's got a job open, that I'm the man to fill it?"

"I can do that. He'll still want to talk to you, though."

"I'll be back, I promise. Come on Abel, let's get up on the mountain 'fore somebody gets up on their high horse and does something stupid."

Chapter Four

Abel and Jesse were the last to arrive at Big Tom McAdoo's cabin. "Cabin" did not do the place justice. True, it had started out, as many domiciles in the area had, as a log cabin. Over the years it had been added to, expanded, and improved. If it hadn't become the biggest house on the mountain it would be a close second. The folks on the other side claimed Garland Lebrun had it beat a mile. All pig slop, of course. That house looked like a tool shed next to Big Tom's, and everybody knew it. Tom McAdoo's house had the further distinction of having had the dirt floor replaced with real planking. The boards squeaked and shifted when you walked on them, but by mountain standards and with a hand-braided rag rug thrown here and there, the floor looked almost decadent.

Men sat or stood in Big Tom's front room, some in front of the small windows that blocked what little light might otherwise have managed to filter in. They shuffled their feet and grumbled and were clearly angry and ready to make a move. They only needed a signal and they would charge out, track down, and kill whoever it was they were convinced had shot their kinsman. An informal consensus deemed that the only people or person likely to have done it would be one of the Lebruns. That family had been at odds with Big Tom's clan for as long as anyone could remember. Some thought the enmity stretched clear back to the Revolutionary War—maybe before that. Certainly they had been feuding for as long as either family could remember being on the mountain and that was a long, long time. Except for the duration of the Civil War, when both sides had rallied to the "Stars and Bars," a cause to which they all subscribed, the east side of the mountain and the west had never got along, even though over the years, the families had intermarried here and there, and probably had more in common than either would admit.

Big Tom was in full voice when they entered. "It seems pretty much a done thing," he said. "It had to have been one of the Lebruns. The way I see it, they found out where it was and Solomon must have caught them busting up my still and tried to stop them. They got into a tussle and they shot him in the back like the cowards they are, and that's that."

Jesse surveyed the gathering. In his lieutenant's uniform, he'd been a commanding presence. Among his relations and in a worn homespun shirt and overalls, not so much. Still, he had their respect.

"Big Tom, you don't know that. It sounds right, but there's no evidence that it went that way. If we all go out Lebrun-hunting, a whole lot of folks is going to be hurt or killed. I say call the sheriff and let him sort this out."

"Now, Jesse, you know good and well, we don't cotton to no flatland lawman coming up here."

Jesse opened his mouth to respond, But his cousin spoke up. Anse McAdoo shook his fist at Jesse. "I'm surprised that this old war hero is turning out to be such a rabbit. Everybody in this room knows who shot Solomon. We need to get on over to the other side of the mountain and hold them to account for what they done. What are you feared of, Jesse?"

"The only thing scares me is when some cork brain gets to mouthing off about something he don't know diddly-squat about. What possible reason can anyone have for not letting the law do its business?"

"You been away playing soldier too long, Cousin. You done forgot who you are."

"I ain't forgot nothing, sonny."

"No police. They won't look for a killer until after they bust up our stills," Big Tom said.

"Okay, we ask the preacher to look into it."

"That old hen couldn't find the privy with a map."

If anybody in the room had a nodding acquaintance with Shakespeare and *Julius Caesar* which, of course, no one did, Anse McAddo would have been compared to Cassius. Lean and hungry, that was Anse. He'd been shifting back and forth from one foot to the other. "I've had enough of this pussy footing around. Are we going to settle this with the Lebruns or are we going to listen to this man who must have had all the grit knocked out of him by them Frenchies? I bet he must've spent all his fighting time over there in a bawdy house."

"I spent all my time over there in a muddy trench with bad food and death around every damned corner. It ain't that I lost my grit, Anse, I lost my taste for killing someone just because I could."

"Well, I say you've come back an old woman and there's the end to it."

"Judas Priest, I come home having survived shelling by Big Bertha, mortar rounds, Mauser bullets, trench fever, mustard gas, cooties, typhus, dysentery, mud, and gore, and I have to sit here and be assaulted with cow flop thrown at me by this pup? I ain't having it, Grandpa. You tell your boy over there to shut his mouth or I'll shut it for him."

Anse stood and balled his fists. "You and your soldiering. You think 'cause you got yourself a medal and fancy uniform you're better'n the rest of us. Well, it ain't true. I could have gone over there if I had wanted. Ain't nothing so special about that."

"But you didn't, did you? You disappeared in the woods 'til everybody left, the way I hear it."

Big Tom banged his fist down on the table. "That's enough, Jesse. And you sit down, Anse. You ain't got no complaint here except you don't like standing in your cousin's shadow. You need to move off and make your own way, you hear? Anyway, we need to sort out who kilt Solomon. We get done with that and then you can try out your wings on Jesse, but if I were you, I'd think twice 'fore I took that on."

Anse glowered at his grandfather and sat. "This ain't over."

Jesse took a breath, shook his head to clear it and turned back to continue his thought. "Look, I don't know who shot old Solomon. He's my cousin, too. Ain't that right? Me and him spent time in French mud together getting shot at. What we shared over there can't be put to a measure and it made us closer than cousins—more like brothers. That's the way it goes when you share a war. I will be the first one in line to see whoever killed him hanging from a gallows, but the one thing I learned sitting in the mud in France, and that is, things ain't always what they seem. That's all I'm saying. We just don't rightly know who pulled the trigger and until we do, I say wait. Why is everybody so fired up to go out shooting? It's not glorious, I tell you. It's mean. By damn, we lost about twelve thousand men over there in less than a year fighting folks who had no more idea why they was there than we did. Some duke or something got killed by one of his own and the next thing you know submarines are sinking liners and we are off to fight a war that had nothing to do with Buffalo Mountain, the State of Virginia, or the U. S. of A. I'm saying let's just all of us sit back a minute and think this thing through."

"Come on, Jesse, you know as well as the rest of us, it had to be the Lebruns. They been after us for years."

"I do know that. I know they're sneaky, and dishonest, and would cheat their own grandma if they got a chance. On the other hand, I know they ain't stupid. Killing one of us could only mean we'd sit down, like we are doing right this very minute, and decide to kill one or two of them. I just don't think they'd do that. They know as sure as Sunday comes after Saturday, that if they did, we'd be on them like flies on horse shit. Would a Lebrun kill one of us in a shootout if they thought they were threatened? Sure they would and so would we. Would they shoot you in the back at one of those? They would if they could. But cold blooded murder? No, it don't make sense. Like I said, they ain't stupid and they are not interested in getting shot any more than we are."

Men murmured and shot angry looks at Jesse. They didn't like to think that Jesse might have called them cork-brained and, anyway, their blood was up and they were dead set on doing something, even if it was the wrong thing. Uncle Bob Knox stood and signaled for silence.

"I hear what Jesse is saying. I ain't saying I agree with him, no sir, but he has a point. Think a minute. Them Lebruns ain't going nowhere. We can shoot them as easy tomorrow or the next day as today. So, I say give Jesse a chance to work this out his way. If he can't get that done in, say, four days, then we go get us some Lebruns."

Men started to argue and shout. Big Tom heaved his bulk from his chair. "Everybody hush up. Here's what we do. First, Jesse, I ain't having no police on my place. They take one look at that still and figure, rightly, it ain't the only one hereabouts, we none of us will see daylight except between bars for six months, give or take, and whoever shot Solomon will get off scot free. So, second, Jesse, if you can sort this out your way, fine. It will give me more time to clean my brand-spanking new repeating rifle. That's it. It's on your head, Jesse. You have yourself four days."

Chapter Five

Solomon's body had been carried to his mother's house hours earlier. An attempt had been made to set the still and the keg back on their bases, although it would be days, maybe a week, before Big Tom would have it working again. Most of the contents of the thump keg and kettle had washed down the creek. Jesse surveyed the scene and tried to reconstruct what it might have looked like before all that had been done.

"Where was Solomon lying, exactly?"

Jesse's grandfather walked to a spot next to the creek. "Right about here. He was lying facedown and his head was nearly in the water."

"Umm. And the still was all busted up and lying next to him?"

"No, more like in front of him in the creek. Them Lebruns... okay, okay, like you say, we don't know for sure, whoever it was shot Solomon... They must have shoved the whole caboodle in the creek. He come up on them, says something, and he turns to get help. They get scared and they shoot him in the back, so he can't."

"If that were the way it went, Solomon should have been lying over there a dozen yards in the other direction. How'd he end up by the water?"

"Hell, I don't know, Jesse. Maybe they drug him over or something."

"Why would anybody except a crazy person, even bother with that? Grandpa, listen. You said you sent him up here to tend the fire. So, let's say he was standing about here." Jesse took a position a few yards from the still. "Somebody sneaks up behind him and shoots. He falls forward and knocks all the apparatus over into the creek. Don't that work better?"

"It does. The problem I see, though, is why shoot him? He weren't in anybody's way. If busting the still was the plan, all they had to do would be wait 'til he went home and they could do that and nobody'd be the wiser."

"Exactly."

"So? Why?"

"I, honest to God, do not know. That is what I aim to find out. Poor Solomon. He deserved a better hand than he was dealt."

"Yep. Um…Jesse, was he, you know, a coward in the war?"

"Solomon a coward? Why would you think that?"

"Well, he come back all shaky and like to go to pieces when a loud noise or a gun went off out of his sight. You seen that."

"I did. Listen, Grandpa, when it came time to go over the top—that's what they called climbing out of that gol-'durned trench, and charge across No Man's Land—Solomon would be the first to go. He fought like a crazy man."

"But all that loony business…"

"It's what they call shell shock. Try to imagine this. You're hunkered down in a trench 'bout ten or twelve feet deep. That is in front. In the back trenches where the reserves was at and such, maybe not so deep. Anyway, say the brass hats is planning to attack, or maybe the other side is, or maybe just hoping to kill a bunch of us. So they start by lobbing in mortar rounds. That goes on for an hour. We send some back. Explosions, here, there, everywhere for hours and hours. It stops, 'Whew," you say. 'We can get us some rest now.' You ease back and it starts all over only this time some sauerkraut-eater six miles away starts lobbing in artillery shells from one of the big damned howitzers they have. Then maybe their cannons would try to blast your parapets down. Grandpa, this could go on for hours and get repeated for three, four nights, in a row, maybe a week. Imagine it…" Jesse pivoted and pointed to various spots in the surrounding woods. "Boom, ka-pow, ba-boom, a-a-a-a, maybe a whiz-bang or two come in. They scare the hell out of you. You only hear them a second before they explode and it's too late to find a hole to hide in. All this goes on over and over again, hour after hour. Men cracked. Good men. Brave men."

"You didn't."

"No, I didn't. I come close a time or two. I guess I'm just too stupid to know any better. See, here's how it was. We all knew that soon or late, we was going to die. Out there in the dark was a bullet with your name on it. Every single one of us, English, French, them Canadians and Aussies, everyone thought, 'I'm going to die.' That's a certainty we all figured on, you know? We just didn't know when. And if that bullet or piece of shrapnel didn't kill you right off, the gangrene would. It were like that every damned day, see? Every damned day, Grandpa, every damned day! Men broke. Some went back for a rest and done a little better after that. Solomon? He just never got over it. He wasn't a coward, Grandpa, he was a casualty."

Big Tom stared at the ground for a minute He scuffed his feet on the grass. "Poor soul. Well, I reckon he's at peace now."

"Yep. Hard way to find it, though."

"Four days, Jesse. You got four days." Big Tom turned and walked away.

"Yes, sir, I know."

Jesse contemplated his grandfather's retreating back for a moment. Then he began to walk the perimeter of the area. The still had been set up in a natural clearing. Some new pine and mountain laurel made dense under-foliage between tall, fast-growing tulip poplars. The still would be invisible from outside.

He knelt, even stretched out flat on the ground for a minute. He picked up a branch, stripped off its limbs, and began poking the bushes. He studied a patch of ground behind one of them. He wished he had one of those newfangled Brownie cameras from the Kodak people that some of the men had brought to the war. Of course, he'd have to come up with the two dollars one cost, and then there'd be more money to get the pictures delivered or whatever they did. No matter. It wasn't going to happen. He was busted and hadn't a notion where you went to get the pictures out of the darn thing anyway. He'd just have to remember what those footprints looked like somehow.

He was sitting on a stump, working out what must have been the angles and locations of Solomon and his attacker, when Abel wandered into the glade.

"Hoo boy, Jesse, there's a passel of folks that is pretty steamed at you right now. I think Cousin Anse is ready to call you out."

"He's all swagger, Abel, like a banty rooster. He's all about strutting and crowing, but ain't much good for anything else. But if he does screw up enough courage to really do something and I ain't died of old age by then, I reckon we'll just have to deal with it. Come over here."

Jesse walked him over to the bushes he'd been studying earlier. He pushed the branches aside with his stick. "What do you see?"

"Foot rints. Any fool can see that."

"Right and you ain't no fool. Whose do you suppose they are?"

"Holy Ned, how am I supposed to know that?"

"They are bare feet, right? And not too big."

"Boys, girls, women? Shorty McCarter's got them really tiny feet."

"And so does Grandpa. We know for sure he didn't shoot Solomon, so for now, it's just feet. So what does it tell us otherwise?"

You got me there, Jesse. All I see is footsteps. Oh, you mean there's two sets."

"That, for sure, yes. Otherwise, the only important thing at the moment, Abel, is they belong to someone who wasn't wearing shoes. If they belong to our shooter, it means one thing. Then again, if they don't, and if they are recent, they'd belong to witnesses. Either way, we know they're local. We find the owners of these feet and we got us a killer."

"That's a bit of a stretch."

"It is, but right now, it's what we got. We're looking for some bare feet, Abel. You study them real good. We're going to have to match them from memory. For example, do you see how that little toe on the left set is squinched over? How many folks hereabouts have a toe like that?"

"You got me there."

"Time to start looking."

Chapter Six

Jesse circled the area one more time and found traces of the footprints he believed were made by the two people leaving the glen. Farther on, they overlapped with what appeared to be the same prints coming from the other direction.

"Come on, Abel, we're going to track us a pair of skunks." They followed scuffed leaves and bent branches through the underbrush to the creekbank. A dozen yards further on, they disappeared. He glanced and the creekbed. "This here is a shallow. I reckon this is where they crossed over. There should be more of the prints on 'tother side." They splashed across the creek and picked up the trail a few yards downstream. The track twisted through the wood until it joined a reasonably marked path. The earth had been packed down hard from the goings and comings of hundreds of feet over the past months and the prints became more difficult to follow.

"Jesse, you see which way they are headed, right?"

"You mean east?"

"Yep and that means Grandpa is right, it has to be the Lebruns."

"Abel, think a minute. One, these prints could sheer off anywhere along this path and we'd never know it. They might even double back. If I was a shooter and just killed somebody, I surer'n hell would make a beeline to where I'm going to hole up. Unless these prints belong to a pair of idiots, figuring the way they're headed is telling you where they're going ain't worth a Confederate ten dollar bill. Two, do you know anybody except Lebruns who live over on the east side? 'Course you do. There's Barkers and Eveleths, there's Pennys, and Walkers, though I ain't so sure about them as being necessarily innocent. There's all sorts of folks over there who have a problem with all of us who're related to McAdoos."

"Well, sure there is, but none of them is a likely shooter."

"No? The trouble with this whole family is we got Lebruns on the brain. Something goes wrong in our lives, it must be the Lebruns causing it. We lose a two-bit piece, the Lebruns must have stole it. A tree falls down in the road, Lebruns pushed it over. Bad as they are, man and boy, they ain't the only skunks in the woodpile. I want them to be guilty as much as the next man, but I want to be sure it's them before I start throwing lead their way."

"Gol' by damn, I swear, Jesse, you are the most pig-headed man in the whole durn state."

"Maybe I am. But I will not be the horse led to the glue factory for bucking off the wrong rider. You think about it."

Abel raised his hands in the air. "Jesse, what's to think? We have to stand together."

"Abel, listen to me. You do not want to end up a sad old man on this mountain. I don't reckon I'll ever find my way off, but you're young and got opportunities. Chose them, not 'I'm a McAdoo, I let someone else do my thinking for me.' Be your own self."

"Jesse, I don't understand. Living here is the best, for sure."

"No, Abel it is the second-worst place I ever lived."

"The second?"

"Them trenches was a hundred times worse. This is not the life you want. It don't lead anywhere. You know that old railroad track they built when the logging was big business? A train ain't rolled on it in forty years, but it's still there. You know where it leads? Nowhere. It is a dead end. Life on this mountain is like that. It will get you nowhere, Abel. It's from another time and it ain't going get you anyplace except old, and tired, and broke. You don't want to end your days scratching a living off of land that played out fifty years ago or running moonshine, maybe going to jail and, worst of all, living in ignorance like a blind pig rooting for acorns, just like your brother and cousins. Don't do it. Get out."

They spent the next hour in an unsuccessful attempt to pick up the trail of footprints. By mid-afternoon Jesse admitted they'd hit a wall. By then the scowl that Jesse's tirade had put on Abel's face had disappeared. Everyone knew he loved his brother, but sometimes, the folks who knew him best, wondered about Jesse. Must have been the war that turned him.

Jesse sent his brother on home. He wanted some time alone. Too much time with Abel and he found himself ready to smack him along side of his head. He loved his brother and he worried about him. There were times when that boy like to drive him crazy. Of all the clan, Abel had a chance to be something more than just another mountain yokel. The city slickers had a name for people like him and Abel. During boot camp, some men from up north called Solomon and Jesse "hillbillies." They did so for two or three days until Jesse walked them behind the barracks one evening before taps. The next morning four recruits from New Jersey showed up for inspection with shiners the size of flapjacks. "Hillbilly" disappeared from the vocabulary of Company B from that day on. But, if he was honest, Jesse knew that hillbillies was exactly what they were—backward, ignorant, and slow-thinking men who would be used and ill-used throughout their lives by people with power and money. Jesse figured he could manage alright, but his younger brother deserved a better life than that. Jesse hoped it wasn't too late.

He found a fallen tree trunk and sat. Some birds sang in a tree nearby and a light breeze stirred the leaves. Light filtered through the canopy of new growth trees and at that moment, Jesse thought, if this was all there was to living on the mountain, then maybe Abel had it right. The simple truth, however: it wasn't like this. It was hard and cruel and uncertain. He pulled his thoughts back to his problem. There was something all wrong about Solomon's killing, but he couldn't put his finger on it. If it had been anyone else, you might be able to put a cause-and-effect story together, but Solomon was a lost soul, a threat to no one in any way, shape, or form. People ridiculed him, but no one disliked him. So, why kill him? Why not Big Tom, or Anse, or him, even? Anse McAdoo had been begging for a bullet ever since he learned to talk, and not just from the Lebruns.

Jesse needed someone to talk to. In the Army, he'd discovered that when he spoke a plan out loud to someone, he could right off hear the problems in it. Who would listen to him talk? None of his relatives, for sure. They would just start arguing with him and hollering "Lebruns musta done it." It was like they had ear wax so bad that was the only word that got through. He looked skyward to estimate the time. A little past three, if he figured it right. If he hurried, maybe he'd be lucky and get to the mill before R.G. Anderson got back from Roanoke. then maybe Serena Barker would hear him out. Women, he had to admit, made better listeners than men, except maybe preachers. Though this latest preacher that headed up the little church down near the road wasn't one of them that did. Serena, on the other hand, would. He hoped she would, anyway.

He stood and made his way back down the mountainside toward the road and the mill. He made sure that none of the McAdoos or the associated families saw him.

Chapter Seven

As it happened, R.G. Anderson had returned from Roanoke and now occupied a desk in the corner behind Serena. She had not moved except she'd taken off her hat and had donned black sleeve stockings. She looked up at Jesse through lowered eyelids and thick lashes. Jesse thought he spotted a hint of a smile. No doubt about it, she was a looker. He paused at the doorsill, unsure how to proceed. Having a chat with her about killings and retribution was not going to happen now. R.G. leaned forward and squinted through his thick glasses.

"Is that Jesse Sutherlin?"

"Yes, sir, it's me alright."

"Well, look at you. War sure seemed to have done you some good. All that marching and such. Gotta build a man's character and body, ain't that right? I think being a soldier should be every able-bodied man's duty. I'm just heartbroke my bad eyes kept me from the action over there. Boy, I bet you shot a passel of them German devils, didn't you?"

"I can't rightly say, Mister Anderson. It's a pretty confusing time when folks is shooting and the cannons are going off right and left."

"Now, I now you're just being modest. Here, sit down. Miss Barker tells me you would like a job here at the mill. Is that right?"

"Yes sir, I would. I'm a good worker and a quick learner and—"

"I ain't worried none about that. You served in the war. Boys like you need to be took care of. So, how's stepping in as foreman sound?"

"Foreman? Mister Anderson, I worked this mill for one summer when I was fifteen. What I learned then don't qualify me to be a foreman."

"Nonsense. It isn't a complicated business. The sawyers have all been doing their job for all their growed up lives. You just nudge them along, that's all. Here, Miss Barker will walk you around. You have a word or two with the men, look at the layout, then comeback and we'll sign you on. Alrighty, Missy, up and at 'em."

Serena stood and pulled the sleeve protectors free, retrieved her hat, and started toward the door.

"Follow me, Mister Sutherlin." She pointed toward the door and gifted him with a grin.

When they were well away from the office building, Jesse turned to her. "What in all that's holy is your boss going on about? I ain't no foreman."

"That's where you are wrong, Jesse. Okay, there're two things you have to consider here. Number one, you don't have to know a whole lot to boss these men around. It helps if you can show a new hire how to do his job, but it's not that important. What is important is the men have to respect you and know they can trust you, know you will stand with them. You do all that, and you can be the foreman. You were an officer in the Army, isn't that right? Same thing. Besides, most of these boys, they're pretty set in their ways and they'd rather not take on the responsibility."

"Okay, maybe that's true. What's number two?"

"Two? Oh, two, Mister Anderson is a hero worshipper. He wanted to sign up for the war but he's, like, blind as a bat without his specs. He heard about some of your doings over there in France and he, I don't know, wants to stand in your shine, I guess."

"Stand in my…he don't have a notion what went on over there, does he? He's one of those flag waving, 'War is heroic and grand,' people ain't he?"

"That isn't fair, Jesse. It's just that he joined up as a boy when we fought the Spaniards. He said he was with Roosevelt on Kettle Hill. Back then his eyes weren't so bad, I guess, and besides, Teddy Roosevelt had bad eyes then, too, so I guess they were okay with that. They told him this time he was too old and his eyesight too bad and turned him down. Anyway, Jesse, the newspapers were all filled up with stories written by men who claimed they were over there and they did make it sound pretty glorious. You even got a mention now and again."

"Me? What them papers say I did?"

"Well, if I remember right, there was the time you jumped in a German trench and killed all the men who were shooting one of those machine gun things and took a slew of prisoners. That was true, wasn't it?"

Jesse sighed and rubbed his eyes. "Some of it, yes. Look, I wasn't no Sergeant York, okay. Sometimes, Serena, you get to doing something and it just sort of swallows you up. I went to scout, it was dark, and I got lost, and fell in the damned—excuse me…fell in that old trench. The Germans were as bowled over as me. Then, it was me taking care of them or them doing me in. The rest just sort of happened. In any case, it ain't something we generally talk about. Most bravery is accidental."

"I don't believe that for a minute. So, you'll take the job, won't you?"

"I'd be crazy as a June bug if I didn't. But I do have a serious question. All of the good timber on this mountain, well most of it anyway, was stripped off forty years and more ago. What's left is new growth and mostly not yet big enough or worth anything as timber. I reckon the poplars might be worth something, but who builds with them? What's he sawing that lets him buy a new car and hire on more hands?"

"There you go. You are a foreman. Smart is what you need to be. You're right. The building trade timber, pine and so on, is gone. In twenty or thirty years we might could timber the mountain again. What's left are the old hardwoods. R.G. got himself a contract to provide walnut, black cherry, and so on, to furniture makers up there in New England and some new ones south. He can afford to cut individual trees if he can buy them cheap enough, and folks on the mountain are happy to see a five-dollar bill for doing nothing. Then, the chestnut blight popped up and is killing off trees all over the place. The trees are dead from the roots going rotten, but the wood up top is good. He aims to cash in on what he is calling a 'botanical disaster.' Also, he's cutting thin for veneers and that newfangled thing they're calling plywood. That means running the eight-foot blade and cutting big sheets. He's busy, Jesse. He needs you."

"He might be blind as a bat, like you say, but he ain't stupid."

They walked the limits of the sawmill operation. He checked the sheds, the planers, steam engines, and the new tractors being installed to replace some of the older steam equipment. He chatted with the men, some he knew, some knew him. What he'd done as a teenager came back to him. Nineteen fifteen had been a hard summer. Money was near non-existent and he'd worked at the mill for fifty cents a day. He'd been put on every dangerous piece of equipment on the lot and nearly lost a couple of fingers on the V-track when the carriage carrying a log at least three feet in diameter rolled forward to the blade before he expected it.

They turned the corner of the office building and Serena made a move toward the door.

"Serena, listen, can you give me a couple of minutes? I need to talk about something and it's not sawing logs."

"Well, R.G. didn't say how long this tour needs to be, so why not? Let's go over to the new log stack. There's some shade and privacy there. You do need privacy, right?"

"It would be a big help, yeah."

He filled her in on Solomon's shooting and how the entire west side of the mountain had its blood up to take out revenge on the Lebruns in general.

"Without proof?"

"The McAdoos been fussing with the Lebruns for over a hundred years, Serena. It's in the blood, I guess. Nobody's looking for proof."

"And you agree?"

"Not with shooting them on a 'maybe,' no, but as a general rule, probably."

"Then you'd have to start with me."

"No, you ain't one of them."

"Jesse, you know how this all works. If you're related, you're one of them. Look at you. Your name is Sutherlin, but you're a McAdoo. Your Uncle Bob Knox married a Finch,who is Big Tom's sister's girl and that makes him a McAdoo. So, my older brother married Sally Stinchcomb whose folks don't even live here, but her brother married Elva Lebrun. They moved to Picketsville two years ago but that don't matter and because of that, it makes me and Jake, my younger brother, a Lebrun. If my mother and father had outrun the Spanish flu, they'd be Lebruns, too. It's silly and stupid, but it is the way we do things here. Everybody has got to be one of them, or one of us. You see how this whole family business goes? So, Jesse Sutherlin McAdoo, are you fixing to shoot me?"

"Course not. You've pegged it and I want this 'we hate them Lebruns' thing to go away. How can I do that if I can't sit down face-to-face and talk it out?"

"You can start by taking to me."

Chapter Eight

"Here's the part I don't understand, Jesse. History or not, what keeps the hatred between the two clans alive? I can understand if one person hurts another and it doesn't get sorted, folks would have a problem that might hang on for a while, but after a time, it should go away. This division between us, like you say, is historic and mostly lost in time. Does anybody remember how it started or why? And another thing, why is it anyone else's business?"

"How do I hate thee? Let me count the ways…"

"That's not how it goes."

"Not how what goes?"

"The poem. It's *'How do I love thee? Let me count the ways.'* It's one of Elizabeth Barrett Browning's poems."

"I had no notion it was a poem. Is it really? What I heard was this big man from out in Illinois or Indiana someplace reciting it while he groused about his situation. He spent a year or two as a college man so maybe he knew that poem, I don't know, only he'd say something like, 'Sergeants,' or 'Trenches,' or 'Germans,' and then go on with, 'How do I hate thee, let me count the ways' and he'd start numbering all the things that was wrong about whatever it was he had in mind. We all thought it was funny at first and we'd chime in with our contributions to the list. After a while, though, it got to be a mite tiresome and toward the end, there, when he'd start in on his "How do I hate thee?' we'd tell him using words I can't rightly repeat here, to hush up or someone would throw something at him."

"Oh, I see. Well, it's a mighty pretty poem and I hate to hear it fooled with like that."

"So, how does it go?"

Serena reached into her pocket and removed a slim book. "Mister Conklin gave me this book when I graduated ninth grade. He said I should stay in school. He said, "Serena, you are too bright to be submerged"...that's how he put it, 'submerged... into the mountain.' Ain't that something? He gave me this collection of her poems. I carry it around and read at it from time to time. Don't look at me that way. It's a woman thing. They're called, *Sonnets to the Portuguese* and that one is number forty-three." She turned the pages and read.

How do I love thee? Let me count the ways.
I love thee to the depth and breadth and height
My soul can reach, when feeling out of sight
For the ends of being and ideal grace.
I love thee to the level of every day's
Most quiet need, by sun and candle-light.
I love thee freely, as men strive for right.
I love thee purely, as they turn from praise.
I love thee with the passion put to use
In my old griefs, and with my childhood's faith.
I love thee with a love I seemed to lose
With my lost saints. I love thee with the breath,
Smiles, tears, of all my life; and, if God choose,
I shall but love thee better after death.

"And that was a poem this woman wrote to a Portuguese feller?"

"No, I think it was a love poem she wrote to her husband, only before they were married, or something."

"Why'd she say it was to the Portuguese?"

"No idea, Jesse. Poets are peculiar people, I guess."

"Portuguese need all the help they can get, I reckon. They were on the line and they run out of reserves. Their government must have not been so committed to the war so they left them up there for like a long time. Some of them people were at the front for months. Everyone else rotated, you know?"

"I have no idea what you are going on about. So what is it you need to do to stop an all-out war on the mountain?"

"I need to find out who shot Solomon and get him in front of the sheriff before someone on our side does something really stupid against someone on your side. I need to have a face-to-face with someone over on the east side of the mountain who feels the same as me and will help settle this."

"In front of the sheriff? You have a problem right from the git-go."

"Which is?"

"Nobody on the mountain is going to call a police. You know as well as I do that they hate them as much as they hate each other."

"Maybe so, but...you could ask around."

"Me? Jesse, you are sometimes the smartest man out here and then you say something that makes me believe you are thick as oak. Me? You heard R.G. back there. I am not Miss Barker. I am not Serena. At work or back home, I am 'Missy' or, 'you, girl,' or just, 'woman.' Nobody is going to listen to me."

"That ain't right."

"It's what it is. Jesse, it was only this past August women got the right to vote. Where you been all your life?"

"Except for a little visit to the mud of France, right here on this very same mountain, Serena. So, what am I going to do? In four days, if I don't come up with something, there's going to be shooting. People are going to be hurt, people are going to die. And some of the shooters are going to be happy for the mess they create. The worst of it is that the person who actually shot Solomon probably won't be the one killed."

"Won't? Why not?"

"What're the chances he's still here? If I was him, I would be halfway to Tennessee by now."

"Oh."

"Oh is right, and anybody with a brain big as a black-eyed pea could figure that out, but that won't stop some hothead from trying to settle the score by perforating the next best thing, which would be the first Lebrun who crossed his path. Then there'd be no stopping it 'til we're all dead or in jail."

"I could talk to my brother. He'll listen to me, and maybe you and him could work this out. It's worth a try."

"That'd be great. Can you do that? Meantime, I will get back to the creek and poke around some more. Maybe I can find something better than footprints that'll tell me the who or the why of the shooting."

"You found footprints? Anything special about them?"

"Just a funny toe on one set. Oh, and they're smallish."

"My feet are smallish. Maybe I did the shooting."

"Let me see your hands."

"My hands? Not my feet? Why?"

"Hold them out." Serena did as he asked. He took them in his, turned them over and then, before she could stop him, he held them to his face.

"What are you doing, Jesse Sutherlin? You're getting mighty familiar." She gave him a look and jerked her hands away.

"You didn't shoot anybody recently, Serena. You are officially off the list of suspects."

"Well, thank you for that. You haven't answered my question. What was that all about?"

"Gunpowder leaves a coating on your hands when you shoot. These old guns we got back here in the mountains is famous for smoke and dirt. Ain't you ever noticed? Anyway, your hands are clean and I can't smell any gun smoke on them. That's what I was doing, sniffing your hands. They smell mighty nice, by the way."

Serena took a swing at him. He ducked and laughed. "No need to get all worked up. It was your idea."

She shook her head and settled her hat back on her head. "I reckon we'll be needing to get back. You have a paper to sign and I got work to do."

They made their way back toward the office.

"So, you really carry that poetry book with you all over the place?"

"I do. Is that a problem for you, Mister Sutherlin?"

"Nope, just different."

"Different how?'

"Most of what I expect to find in a pocket is some coins, a chew, or a six-shooter."

"Women don't go in for any of those things except maybe the coins. We'd rather have a pocket square, a book, or a sprig of mint."

"And they give y'all the vote. Lord have mercy."

Chapter Nine

It took longer to travel to Jesse's house by road than if he elected the shortcut. A path cut straight through the woods to the cabin his great grandfather had built and in which he, his mother, and brother lived. Jesse's father and a companion had ventured to Norfolk the previous year and in that strange urban mix, had contracted the Spanish influenza that had killed off hundreds of thousands around the world. The influenza pandemic had waned considerably by then. Indeed, Norfolk officialdom had declared that for all practical purposes, it was over, except for one very vulnerable stranger from the wilds of the Blue Ridge. His friend returned alone with the news of the death and the worse news that he had not had the fifty dollars the undertaker wanted to ship the body home. Jesse's father occupied an anonymous grave in Norfolk. Addie had never had the time or resources to visit it. One or two others on the mountain had succumbed as well, but the mountain's relative isolation had spared it from the worst of the global epidemic.

The path climbed straight up the mountain and could be accessed by a man on foot or on a horse or mule, but the angle of incline made wagon and, nowadays, car traffic, next to impossible. The road wandered around the side of the mountain for a mile or so and circled past the house. Jesse steered the T-Model carefully off the road and around Blue, the coon hound, sleeping in the middle of the yard and jerked to a halt. Abel, who'd been watching his approach, scrambled off the porch and ran to greet him

"Whoo-ee, what are you doing in that automobile? Is that Mister Anderson's? Why are you driving it? Jesse, how'd you come by that? Holy cow."

"That is a bucket full of questions, Abel. So, here is how it happened. You remember I went to the mill to get a job? Well, I went back there this afternoon and Mister R.G. Anderson made me foreman. It pays twice what I would have made doing the heavy work. Then he says, 'Jesse, I want you to be mobile.' That's how he put it, 'mobile.' Then he says, 'Here's what we can do. I will sell you my old Ford for twenty-five dollars.' I say, 'R.G., I ain't got twenty-five dollars.' He says, 'I'll keep back two dollars a week from your pay 'til it's paid off.' So here I am. I have me a good-paying job, an automobile, and here's the best part. He's replacing some of the old steam tractors that power the mills with those big Allis-Chalmers 6/12 gasoline tractors. He even had a big tank to hold gasoline set up on the property for his trucks and the new tractors and says I can fill up this old flivver from it and it won't cost me a red cent."

"He made you a foreman?"

"He did."

"And sold you his old car?"

"Yep."

"Golly. Kin I drive it?"

"Nope. Maybe someday. You are a mite too short on years, I think. When you're sixteen next December, you can. You'll have to learn the pedals and such. It ain't as easy as it looks."

"You can do it."

"Yes, I can on account I learned how to in the Army. They used big old Mack trucks on the base and made everybody learn how to drive them. I reckon they thought we'd have them in France. The Brits had a bunch, I heard, and some other units had them and even tried out their armored car, but they never got to us. Anyhow, if you can drive one of those monsters, you can drive damned near anything."

Addie Sutherlin stepped out of the house and surveyed the boys and sniffed at the car. "Supper's on," she said and turned on her heel.

"Ma don't seem impressed."

"Nope. She is having a hard time fitting in to this new world we got ourselves."

They entered the house and sat.

"It ain't much," his mother said. "Greens and pone, and a scrap of fatback. So, you bought yourself a motor car." It wasn't a question.

"I did and that ain't all. Starting tomorrow, I am full-time working at the mill. It will pay me good money and so, you need to write me up a list of things you need, Ma. You know, flour, butter, sugar, things like that."

"You thinking I'm going to bake a cake? We have all we need right here on the place."

"Ma, we have enough. We aren't going to starve, but there're things that can make life easier. Maybe we can get the roof fixed up. Me and Abel can do it, but how about some real shingles instead of tar paper and tin? Maybe a real bed for you or one of them iceboxes. Ma, I'm working and that means we have us some breathing room when it comes to money."

Addie Sutherlin had lived her entire life on the mountain. Scratching out an existence from the unforgiving earth was all she knew. The idea she might have something more struck her as incomprehensible. Jesse might as well have been speaking Greek.

"Humph," was all she would say.

"What did you learn about Solomon's killer?" Abel said.

"I been chatting with Serena Barker and she said she'd try to set me up with some of the folks on the other side. I think we need to talk before we jump. I'm meeting her later this evening."

"Serena Barker is a Lebrun," Addie said. "Can't trust any of them."

"She's a Lebrun the way your cousin who lives over in Danville and never once set foot on the mountain is a McAdoo. Come on, Ma. Do we really want to start a war like the Hatfields did over in West Virginia?"

"I'm just saying for your own good. Ain't nothing good ever come from—"

"Nazareth, I know. It's in the Bible."

"That wasn't what I was going to say, you smart aleck, and you know it. Besides, where in tarnation am I going to get ice for that box?"

"Now you're talking."

• • ● • •

Jesse had arranged to meet Serena by the old Spring House on a tract of land that had once been called The Oaks and was thought to have belonged to Fitzhugh Lee. Legend had it that Lee'd built himself a hideaway on the mountain. That was the rumor. The facts of the matter were muddied by the number of men who, at the turn of the century, felt compelled to claim a familial tie to the Lees of Virginia and Maryland. The actual ownership remained a mystery. In any event, all that remained of the estate was the Spring House. It served as neutral ground. A kind of No Man's Land, Jesse thought. Neither McAdoos nor Lebruns claimed it as their own.

Serena waited for him in the shadow of an old black walnut tree. Jesse waved and without realizing it, began to size up the tree into useable lumber of various lengths, thicknesses, and widths. He smiled.

"Something funny, Jesse Sutherlin?"

"No. I was walking up here to say hi and even though I ain't spent a day in my new job, I was counting the profit in that tree."

"You could, if you knew whose property it stood on. There's a dozen of these trees around here but nobody has yet figured who of the hundreds of Lee decedents, real and imaginary, it rightly belongs to. You figure that out and R.G. will probably give you the Ford for free."

"Okay, I'll get right on that. What have you got for me otherwise?"

"I had a word with my brother. He thinks you're plumb crazy to take this on, by the way. I agree with him on that score. He says reasonable conversations between us and you-all is a dream. I said, more like a nightmare."

"There's a *but* in there somewhere."

"But, he said the news about your cousin being shot made the rounds and nobody over there knows anything about it. He talked to a bunch from all over, Jesse. They are as ignorant as to who pulled that trigger as you are. You should also know, be warned more like, that they are expecting a gang of McAdoos to ride over and start shooting. They are ready for you, Jesse. There won't be just one dead man when this is over. There'll be a dozen or more."

"I need to talk to someone over there who can help stop this."

"Let's hope you aren't too late."

Chapter Ten

The sun slid down toward the horizon. Jesse turned and studied Serena's profile in the fading light. They'd grown up together as children, but Serena wasn't a child anymore. Back then, they'd been subject to their families' disapproval. "Lebruns and McAdoos don't mix," they'd been told. Still they'd kept up as best they could. When Jesse turned twelve, he'd followed the path most of his contemporaries took and dropped out of school. His father's farm didn't produce much—some corn, potatoes, and beans. The land had played out and modern agriculture practice had not been introduced to the mountain. Nor would it ever be. His father signed on with a timbering operation in the valley and the farming had been left to his sons. In good years, they would have a pig to slaughter and chickens. Local rabbits, opossum, and wild turkeys supplemented the family's protein intake.

Serena's contemporaries, her cousins and neighbors—if they were female they were assumed to be fit only for having babies and taking care of a house, and not much else—had all been married off and some were already facing their third pregnancy. Serena, on the other hand, had been allowed to advance all the way to the ninth grade before the pressure built for her to marry and get on with life. She'd avoided becoming a child bride like the rest because she'd convinced her parents she'd be more useful if she worked at a job. She was an only daughter and the apple of her father's eye and he, to the consternation of his neighbors, had supported her. She'd taught herself how to type, file, and do simple bookkeeping. So now, at the ripe old age of nineteen and still unmarried, she had become the major wage-earner and consequently, the object of local gossip.

"Jesse, you need to get off this mountain," she said.

"Me? I don't think so, Serena. I am stuck here. You maybe can do it. You're smart and can do things that folks will pay you for. I want Abel to get out, but not me. I'm stuck here for the rest of my days."

"That can't be true. Why do you say that?"

"Do you know what the flatland people call us? Hillbillies. I skinned my knuckles a time or two when they threw that at me and Solomon, but you know what? They're right. We are just rubes, yokels, the world's leftovers. We try to hold on to the only way of life we know, but it don't fit into the way things are anymore. We have nothing to offer except being the object of their jokes."

"That's not true."

"It is. Look at me. I can barely read or write. Numbers only add up if they're small. I am just another stupid hillbilly and that's a fact."

"You are not stupid. Ignorant, yes, but not stupid."

"Oh really, Missy? Tell me the difference."

"Ignorant is when you don't know something. That is not a bad thing. It is a…um, a circumstance. You can change that. Stupid is when you are ignorant and are proud of it, when you won't fix it even if you could. You take your cousin Anse or the Lebruns generally. They are stupid."

"I'm not, you think?"

"I think that if you don't know something and you aren't satisfied with that state of affairs, you will go dig out the information. That's the opposite of stupid."

"Unh, huh. Well, that is as may be. Like I say, the only person I want off this mountain is my brother Abel. He can do better."

"Jesse, bless your heart, Abel ain't never going to leave this place. You might as well give up that crusade."

"You're saying he's stupid like the rest of us?"

"Not the rest and not stupid. He's more like, backward."

"Backward? So, the difference is?"

"Okay, stupid is ignorant and proud of it, Backward is ignorant and comfortable with it. Boys and men like Abel are happy where they're at. They fit in like a pebble fits in the creekbed. They will stay wherever God puts them and never complain or look past it. Content."

"You don't think I'm backward?"

"No. Okay, here's a question. We're sitting on a tract of land. There're all sorts of stories about who owns it and so on, but look around you. What do you see?"

"In this light, not much."

"Then, before it got dark, what did you notice?"

"Trees."

"Don't go all pig-headed on me, Jesse. What did you see?"

"Well, there's a pretty good stand of hardwoods here. This tract is supposed to be ten acres and there is maybe ten harvestable trees on each one of them so, there is some money to be made if R.G. could get his hands on the timber rights."

"And?"

"Nobody really knows who owns the land or if the rights is available."

"And?"

"And a trip to the county seat might tell you all that."

"And?"

"And what? You think there's more? If it were me, I hop on over to the courthouse and find out, then…Okay there're two possibilities. Land around here is selling for ten dollars an acre. Ten acres would be worth, um—"

"One hundred dollars."

"Right. So, if it were for sale, and if I could scratch up that kind of money, I'd buy it and then sell the rights to R.G. my own self. I'd more than just get my money back and I'd still have me ten acres of pretty nice land. So, with the board feet I reckon you could take off this pace, I'd get money back four times over.

Maybe even more, depending on how straight the trees is and how many there are. The second case, the land isn't for sale but the rights are, then same deal. Buy and sell."

"There you go. You are not stupid. You are not backward."

"This is a good piece of land, ain't it?"

"Not for farming."

"No, but for living on. You clear out the timber, let the new growth come in. Plant a vegetable patch. It could be nice."

"For some, but not for me. Jesse, I said I think you need to move on. Me too. I am not going to die on this mountain."

"Where, then?"

"I don't rightly know."

"I've seen cities, Serena, Richmond, Baltimore, even Paris, France. They are exciting places for a visit, but I don't want to live in one of them. Once you get past the lights and glitter and look around, you see they are hard places. You can find yourself lost and alone in a crowd. Here you can be poor as dirt, but you have, I don't know, dignity. In the cities, you are also poor, but disposable like trash. If I'm going to die, I want to do it someplace where the air is clear and the water sweet."

"Roanoke?"

"Still too big and the folks there are too much like the folks in the big cities that they want to be like."

"Well, I don't know about you, but wherever I go, it won't mean sleeping in a two-room cabin with a dirt floor and competing with the chickens for the corn."

"You let the chickens eat the corn. Over on this side, the still gets the corn. We compete with the chickens for greens."

They heard a crashing in the brush and Abel stumbled into the clearing, "Holy Ned, Jessie, why'd you pick this spot to go sparking?"

"Sparking? No, we ain't…It's not that. We were talking about what to do with the problem and—"

"If you say so. Grandpa sent me to fetch you. He says you got to come quick. Some of the boys are hooting and hollering about doing something about the shooting. They're fixing to ride on over and who knows what they'll liable to do. They're packing their rifles."

"Who?"

"Well, Anse and them. They found a jug and done got themselves all likkered up and they saying they are going over to the other side of the mountain or get them a Lebrun or two and settle up with them. You have to stop them."

"Me? Where's Grandpa? Where's Uncle Bob?"

"They tried talking to them, but they won't listen."

"And you think they will listen to me?"

"You have to try, Jesse. I ain't against shooting a couple of them that shot Solomon, but drunk shooting is the worst way to go about it. You have to stop them."

"And all the grown-up men can't stop a clutch of drunk boys and they think I can, why is that?"

"Because you are a man who commands respect, is why," Serena said. "You didn't get to be an officer on your good looks and education. Men listen to you, Jesse."

Jesse heaved himself to his feet and turned to Serena. "You might want to hop over to your side of the mountain and tell them folks to lay low for a while. I'll go see if I can slap some sense into Anse and his drunk buddies. You're right. I need to get off this mountain."

Chapter Eleven

It took Jesse nearly twenty minutes to find the clearing where Anse McAdoo and his friends had gathered. Things were considerably worse than Abel had led him to believe. He'd got the drunk and crazy part right. He left out the part about the hostage they'd taken and who now perched on a horse, his hands tied behind his back and a noose around his neck. The rope ran upward and around a branch of an oak tree. Jake Barker was about five seconds away from being lynched.

Jesse stepped to the horse's head and grabbed the lead away from Sam Knox. Sam tried to grab it back and Jesse backhanded him to the ground. He steadied the horse which had begun to sidle. Too far one way or the other and Jake was done for.

"Nobody move." Jesse said and glared at Anse.

"Like I said, this boy ain't got grit," Anse said. His words were slurred. He staggered to the horse's rump and slapped it hard. It was all Jesse could do to hold the beast in place. As it was, it shied and nearly lost its reluctant rider.

"Abel, get over here and cut this man loose."

"Jesse, are you sure?" Abel had counted the number of men in the clearing and he and Jesse were outnumbered five to two.

"Do it and if any of these knuckle-heads give you a hard time, kick them where it hurts. Now cut him loose."

"Goddam traitor," Anse screamed. "You're both traitors. That man's a Lebrun."

"His name is Barker and is as much a Lebrun as your Great-aunt Maudie who, if you remember, was married to Sly Lebrun after the Civil War. Now, Abel, cut him free."

Abel quick-stepped up and sawed through the rope on the Jake Barker's wrist. Once the hands were free, Jake jerked the noose from his neck. Jesse handed him the reins.

"You'd better ride, son, and fast."

"Yes, sir." Jake wheeled the horse and galloped off into the twilight.

"What in hell were you birds thinking? You were going to hang someone because he sort of belonged on other side. You want to go to jail for murder? Are you that stupid?" Jesse remembered Serena's definition of that word and realized he'd answered his own question. "Okay, I reckon you are."

Anse balled his fists and took a step toward Jesse. "I think we should be stringing you up, Jesse Sutherlin. You ain't no McAdoo, no more. You turned that boy loose and that makes you a damned Lebrun. What do you say, boys? Shall we string up this traitor?"

The other four murmured. Abel stepped up close to Jesse. "What're we going to do, Jess?"

"Do? Nothing. These boys haven't the gumption to try anything more complicated than gigging bullfrogs. They are stupid, but not that stupid." He spread his hands wide, palms up. "Okie dokie, which one of you is going to be first?"

"Well, go on, someone," Anse shouted.

Sam Knox jammed his hands in his pockets. "I ain't so sure about this. He learned all that hand-to-hand combat in the Army, Anse."

"There's four of you and two of them and the kid will melt like butter in July."

"Well, boys, what's holding you back? See, I got no knife, no gun, nothing but a mean disposition. And Abel? He's ready to join up with the League of Nations, he's so peaceable. So, who's it going to be?" Jesse leaned first left and then right. "Come on, boys. Lordy, I seen Fritzies with trench foot and a serious case of cooties that had more backbone than you five. You, Anse, you're the leader. Leaders lead. Ain't that right? Instead of prodding these boys like moving cows to the barn at milking time, why ain't you stepping up? Now, I am wondering if all your talk about someone with no grit is you talking about yourself. Am I close?"

Anse glowered at Jesse. Then, realizing he had been set up, reached into his belt and drew a knife. "Well, we'll just see about that." He charged Jesse, his knife held high.

There was a whirl of bodies and Anse landed facedown on the ground, his wrist broken and his knife stuck in the bole of the oak tree from which the lynching rope still dangled.

"Which of you brave lynch mobsters is next?"

Sam Knox took a step forward and thought better of it. The four turned and started to leave.

"Whoa, you all ain't done here. You pick up your brave captain and take him to Big Tom and explain how he got his wrist broke. Miss Emma will put on a poultice and splint it."

They dragged a whimpering Anse McAdoo away into the night. Abel stared wide-eyed and open-mouthed at Jesse. "Lord love a duck," he said after he'd managed to collect himself. "How'd you do that?"

"Do what? You mean separate Anse from his pig sticker? It ain't as hard as it looks, Abel. When someone comes at you with a knife held high, you just duck under it, throw a forearm across the knife arm and slip your other one in behind. Then you yank it backwards, the knife either comes out or the attacker gets his shoulder knocked out of joint. Sometimes both."

"But Anse's wrist was broke, not his shoulder."

"Yeah, well, that's a story for another day."

"Well, then, suppose he didn't come in high like that but had that knife down low, say waist-high?"

"Then you better hope you thought to bring a gun along."

"A gun? You mean shoot the man?"

"Best way I know to handle that situation. Listen, Abel, what you need to learn here is that this mountain has got itself a culture that is not healthy. If you plan to be anything more than another yokel, old and toothless at forty, dead by sixty, you need to do some serious planning about your future. There's better things to occupy you than moonshine, dirt farming, and fighting."

"Aw, now you're joking."

"No, no joke. Okay, you trot on down to Big Tom's and make sure he's getting the true story of what happened up here tonight. You let Anse tell it, and there's no way any good can come of this. He'll have the whole clan armed and marching in an hour. You get on down there and make sure that don't happen."

"What are you going to do?"

"Me? I am going to sit down under this little tree here and wait 'til my heart stops pounding like some out of control Indian tom-tom. Then I am going have me a think. I need to figure out what I have to do next to pinch off this mountain war before it blows the lid off things."

"You were scared?"

"Abel, any time you get in a position where someone is fixing to kill you or carve you up, at least, and you ain't scared, you'd best check your pulse. You're probably already dead. Now, git, and let me ponder a while. I only have three days left."

Chapter Twelve

Work at the sawmill began at six-thirty, rain or shine, summer or winter. Jesse arrived at five-thirty and walked the lot. The trees to be cut into furniture lengths and sizes were stacked separately from those slated for veneer. Jesse knew more about long cuts of various sizes and widths than he did about veneers. He'd need to do some quick learning on that end of the business. He hoped that his lunch break would give him enough time to run the Ford over to the county seat and dig out the deed to The Oaks. If he could find that out, he'd ask Serena to help him figure out how to write up a contract for the timber rights. She'd know because working at the mill she must have seen a slew of them that R.G. had collected over the years.

Jesse had spent several hours the night before sitting under the stars trying to figure out how to deal with the Lebrun mess. Time was ticking away and if he didn't soon come up with an answer the mountain would explode. He understood the reasons for it; old hatreds are the kindling that light up violence. What bothered him was he had no allies. Even Abel would be more than happy to go over to the east side and start shooting. Why, of all the people he knew, had no one backed him up even a little bit?

The trouble with most of the folks hereabouts was they had no idea what real war felt like, no idea what it was like to be shot at by someone dead-set on seeing you die, had no idea how painful the process could be. Jesse carried the memories of the trenches, the horror of corpses and blood strewn across No Man's Land tangled in barbed wire, bleeding and crying for help, gut shot and soon to die because the chances of recovery from such a were slim at best; and realizing that when the day's fighting ended, nothing had been accomplished. Oh, sometimes they'd move forward a hundred yards or so. Most days, it was just killing and being killed.

What his relatives who'd spent the war in the relative safety of the Shenandoah Valley failed to understand was that settling a dispute with a gun accomplished little or nothing. It only led to more shooting and killing. Jesse knew that his war had been labeled "The War to End All Wars." He hoped it was, but he wondered if that would be true. He did not understand diplomacy and had no idea what had transpired at the peace-treaty meetings after he, and the thousands of other soldiers, the survivors, finally shipped home, but he doubted the losers would be happy.

What his kin thought of war, he imagined, would be something closer to a Sir Walter Scott story or maybe Tom Mix settling the West in the flickers. Battles won by the righteous, villains put down by a six-shooter. Jesse knew his kinfolk were neither heroic knights nor cowboys. They more closely resembled the legendary Hatfields and McCoys whose antics had made the news before the turn of the century. That largely fictionalized feud had molded the national consciousness about hill people in ways that might never change and would forever cast them as backward, stupid, and lazy. As much as he hated the label, Jesse had to accept the fact that his kin were hillbillies. He'd fought strangers more than once when it had been applied to him, and yet, here he was discovering that it might be true. How in hell would he ever shift them into doing the sensible thing? He pulled on his gloves and made ready to earn his pay as foreman of R.G. Anderson's mill.

The workers, sawyers, mechanics, loaders, and shifters drifted in, some a little worse for wear. Coffee wasn't all that available even now, over a year after the war shortages. He set them to work reducing the stack of furniture logs to standard lengths and widths. When R.G. arrived he'd ask him for the specifications and then have the planks resawn and dressed into the stock sizes on order.

Serena arrived at seven-thirty. Jesse waved to her. She smiled and pointed to the office door and then at the sun, now well up in the east. She was late? She disappeared inside. He considered following her in when the truck from Smith's Ice House pulled through the gate. Jesse oversaw the loading of sawdust into the truck and then sent the driver in to settle up with Serena. Not much went to waste here.

The air was filled with the singing of the big circular saws, the whine of the planer as it dressed rough-cut lumber into usable boards, and the scent of newly cut timber. Tractor engines roared, steam engines chuffed, and boards falling away from the finished cut slapped onto the carrier. Jesse was lost in the work.

At noon, the whistle on one of the older steam engines sounded. The saws moaned to silence and the men gathered in groups with their lunch pails to eat and smoke. Jesse went into the office. R.G. waved him over.

"Jesse, I need you to run over to the mercantile and pick up these items." He handed Jesse a list of supplies: grease, oil, and metal rasps. "We will need to lubricate all the machinery and sharpen the saw blades over the weekend, right? I have to run into Roanoke this afternoon or I'd do it myself."

R.G. gathered a stack of papers on his desk into a pile and left. Jesse found himself alone with Serena. He thought he liked that.

"Well, where do I start thanking you, Jesse Sutherlin?"

"Pardon?"

"You saved my brother's life last night, I hear."

"More like I saved Anse and his drunk buddies theirs. If they had done Jake in, they'd be swinging from a rope their own selves pretty soon."

"Don't be going all modest on me. You know it's true. Thank you."

"Well—"

"There's more. By now most everybody over on the east side knows what you did. If you need to sit down with any of them... well, almost any...they'd be open to that."

"Can you set something like that up?"

"I can try. You'd better get on your horse, sorry, Ford, if you want to get over to the mercantile and back 'fore lunch break is done."

"That's too bad, because I had it in mind to sit a spell and eat my cornbread and bacon right here with you, Miss Barker."

"Tomorrow. Now, go."

Jesse smiled and left. If he really hurried, he might be able to drop in on the records clerk and find out a thing or two about The Oaks.

Chapter Thirteen

Jesse wore his wrist watch, a novelty for the time and certainly the place. Some of the folks on the mountain owned pocket watches. A few even carried one on days other than Sunday when they were dressed in what passed for finery. He'd received the Elgin trench watch when he'd been elevated to the officer class. It had a stain on its leather strap that he imagined might have been blood. Because of that he believed it probably belonged to one or the other of his late predecessors. He never asked. He'd not worn it since coming home. He had no real need to track the time beyond what the sun told him as it processed from east to west, but now as foreman, time had become a much more important consideration. He gave it a quick glance as he pulled up to the mercantile. He parked the Ford and strode inside. Once there he dropped the list R.G. gave him on the counter. He said he'd be back in half an hour and left it in the hands of the clerk. The courthouse was two blocks further down the road.

There, he asked for the Registrar's Office and was directed down a flight of stairs to the basement. He found the clerk who could help him with a title search in a dimly lit space that reeked of old and moldy paper. He explained what he needed. The clerk nodded and disappeared into the depths of the room that by now he now realized stretched the length of the building and consisted of rows of shelves which held file boxes with paper labels affixed to their ends. Jesse waited as the minutes ticked away. He checked his watch. Maybe it would be okay if he was late getting back. R.G. had to run errands in Roanoke, Serena said. So, most likely he would not be back at the mill for hours.

"Hello? How's it going in there?" he said.

Silence. He checked his watch again. Finally the clerk returned with a piece of foolscap and slid it across the counter.

"That'll be four bits," he said and kept his hand on the paper effectively covering the information written on it.

"Fifty cents for what took you…" Jesse consulted his watch again. "Twenty minutes? That's a dollar and a half an hour. Nobody around here pays that much."

"It's a flat fee, Bub, whether I find what you're after for in five minutes or five days. Fifty cents, if you want to see what's written on this paper."

Jesse dug around in his pockets and counted out four dimes, a nickel, and five pennies. It didn't leave him much, three more quarters, a dime, three pennies, and something he recognized as a Baltimore streetcar token. He slid the fifty cents across the counter and the clerk released the paper. Jesse picked it up. The man had a mighty fine hand, a nice attempt at copperplate, if Jesse remembered it correctly. He squinted hard at the words. Most of them he could make out with moving the paper back and forth. What *entailed* meant wasn't clear nor did the notation declaring that an *endowment* had been established to assure the taxes were paid in perpetuity. Those words made him stop. This paper was a poser, for sure.

"Excuse me, what does all this mean?"

The clerk retrieved the paper, read it, and handed it back. "As near as I can make it out, son, the owner of this property wanted to be sure that, if he was away for a spell, the taxes would still be paid. That endowment fund he set in place in 1868. It's possible he went off to fight Indians or French Mexicans or maybe went to shoot elephants in Africa, or run cattle in Texas. Whatever, he wanted to make sure he didn't lose the land through tax default. Who can tell? In this here case, that fund has been doing that for…" He scratched his head. "…going on fifty-two years. Now ain't that something."

"It is. And the name of the owner was this man whose name you wrote down here?" Jesse planted a finger on the name.

"Yep, only I can tell you right off that that man is by now dead and gone and it doesn't appear he has an heir. If he did, one hasn't come forward to claim the land."

"How can that be? If you all knew he was dead, why wouldn't you notify next of kin or post it like they do in the newspaper?"

"Like I said, that endowment keeps paying the taxes so there was never any reason for the County to notify anybody. I expect he has an heir out there somewhere and the person, if he knew it, would be in here like a shot, but nobody has come. Now, if the taxes were in arrears, well, there's be a notice posted and such and maybe he'd have found out. Nobody likes to lose a piece of land to the tax man, do they?"

"No, I reckon not." Jesse folded the paper in two and shoved it in the pocket that had a button closure. He didn't want to lose it, for sure. He'd show it to Serena and she'd know right off what to do. He thanked the man and climbed back up to street level and the sunlight.

A black Essex sedan had pulled in and parked beside his Ford. The door had some words painted on them. He made two trips into the store and brought out bundles which he stowed on the backseat. Jesse looked more closely at the car next to his. He made out a name and a word he didn't recognize. He turned to retrieve the third and last of his bundles. He tried to sound out the word in his head, hoping it would be one he'd heard somewhere and he'd know what the door signaled. When he returned, the driver of the sedan stood next to his car studying a map.

"You lost, Mister?"

"Lost? No, well, maybe. I am Samuel Schwartz, haberdasher and tailor."

"How do, Mister Schwartz. Do you have a store here in Floyd?"

"In a way, you're looking at it. I am a sort of, how you say, *pedler.* You know but instead of a pack, I have this very nice car filled with some things I am selling here and there. I am looking for a place to rent. A storefront and place where I can settle."

"Peddler. Okay, well this town has haberdasheries. The big one is Gottlieb's. Wait, it ain't Gottlieb anymore on account of the war. Old Gottlieb changed the name to Lord and Lovett. Gottlieb sounded German, you know."

"Do I know? You think being Schwartz won me so many customers?"

"No, I suppose not. So you want to set up in a big city? I expect you'd do real well in New York."

"You know New York?"

"No, never been there. I got all the way up to Washington D.C. on my way to France, and I seen Paree, but they say that it is real busy up there in New York City."

"Busy, sure, and do you have any idea how many tailors and haberdashers there are on the Lower East Side of that city alone? No? Well, I will tell you. If I didn't know better already, I would swear that Moses took a turn for the west in the desert and took the children out of Egypt to New York City."

"What?"

"I am making a joke. Now look at you. You, I think, need a hat. I will give you a nice price. How about a derby? I have things to sell here. I am a *pedler*, yes?"

"Well, that's mighty nice of you, but I don't need a hat. Wore all the hats I care to in the Army, thank you."

"So, what is in your hair?"

Jesse tilted his head and brushed his hair. Sawdust cascaded to the street.

"What is that?"

"I work at the sawmill. That would be sawdust."

"So, you do need a hat. A derby won't work so good there. I have a nice trilby here, two dollars."

"Sorry. I don't have two bucks and if I did, I wouldn't spend it on a hat."

"At least you should try it." Sam brushed the brim with his sleeve and perched the hat on Jesse's head. "Ah! Your sweetheart will love your for it."

"Not for me, not for two dollars, and I ain't got a sweetheart."

"No? Such a pity."

"I can tell you that one place that could keep a haberdasher busy is Picketsville. You could drive up there and see for yourself. You just pick up the Valley Turnpike just west of here and follow it north past Natural Bridge. It's a public road and I reckon if you hop to, you could be there by suppertime."

Chapter Fourteen

Jesse made it back to the mill before R.G. He had his hand on the cardboard box that held half a dozen cans of lubricant and some files used to sharpen the saw blades when a large shadow blocked out the sun. Sheriff Dalton P. Franklin was a big man. Not big or physically imposing as a Greek god or even the heavyweight boxing champion, Jack Dempsey, but big as in too many flapjacks for breakfast. He wore khaki trousers which had a dark olive stripe along the outside seam. His jacket to which his six-pointed star badge was pinned was also khaki and the brass buttons looked like they might pop at any minute. By the looks of it, his jacket had not been washed or cleaned as often as the trousers and they did not quite match. His tie was the same shade of green as the pants stripe and a Sam Browne belt and a campaign hat completed the outfit. He stood with the light at his back, hands on hips, legs spread. The expression on his face was lost with the sun at his back, but if his reputation held, it would be red and arranged to appear somewhere between smug and downright disagreeable.

Jesse started to say something about how imposing that stance was, but at the same time how it made him particularly vulnerable if you were acquainted with the ins and outs of bare-knuckle fighting. Before he could, the sheriff cut in.

"You're Jesse Sutherlin."

"Yes sir, I am that very feller. Excuse me while I unload this pile of merchandise."

"It'll keep. I have some questions for you. How you answer them will determine where you will spend the next hours, days, or years. You got that, Rube?"

Jesse dropped the package back on the seat of the Ford and leaned back against its door.

"Shoot."

"I understand it was you that found a body up in the mountains. Some sport named Solomon McAdoo. Is that right?"

"No sir, it ain't."

"No? I have a witness says it was you."

"Whoever that witness is he has got it wrong."

"Really. My notes here says it were a relative of yours name of Hansel."

"Hansel? You mean like Hansel and Gretel? Sorry I don't know any Hansel."

"No?"

"No."

"It says here he's a cousin of yours. 'Course that don't mean anything up in the mountains, do it? You all are so intermarried it's a wonder you ain't got three eyes and pointy heads. Or maybe drinking moonshine for breakfast has pickled your brains."

"Really? We like to think of it as very strong mouthwash right up there with that Listerine gargle they sell at the pharmacy store. It's something I would recommend you might give a try. Okay. So, my cousin, Anse, that's with no H at the front and no L at the end, told you or your deputy that he saw me discover a body and you're wondering…what? Do you want to know where's it at? Did I kill someone? You need to understand, Anse ain't wrapped too tight and has a fierce hate for me. Can't say why that is so, but he does. I didn't discover a body, Sheriff. My brother can testify that he brought me the news about Solomon's killing right here at this mill."

Serena rounded the corner and stood at Jesse's side. The sound of voices outside had puzzled Serena, she said afterwards and she came to see who was making a ruckus behind the office, stayed to see to it that Jesse didn't end up in jail for assaulting an officer of the law.

"I was here when that happened. Jesse's telling the truth, Sheriff."

"Yeah? And just who the hell are you, Missy?"

"My name is Serena Barker. I work here for Mister R.G. Anderson. I can tell you straight off, Jesse was sitting in the office when his brother told him the news."

"Of course you can because I reckon you're a 'cousin,' too?"

"Nope. Not even close. Not yet, anyway." Serena stared at Jesse and pointed at him and then to his head, her eyebrows halfway up her forehead. Jesse smiled and tipped his new hat.

"Bought it off a Jewish man in town. He wanted two dollars but I got him down to eighty-eight cents. Didn't even want it at first, but he was convincing."

"Eighty-eight cents? What kind of a number is that?"

"It's all I had left in my pocket after I paid two bits for the title search."

"Well, it does look smart, Jesse Sutherlin. I'll say that. You searched the title of The Oaks?"

"I did."

"What's it say?"

The sheriff's face had acquired a deeper shade of red. "Would you two just let go of hats and titles and listen?"

"Sorry. Was there something else?"

"Goddamn it. If I get any more guff out of you, you'll spend the night in jail."

"Would that include me, too?"Serena asked and shot Jesse a grin.

"You? You just skedaddle, Missy, 'fore I take it in my head to give you a spanking, girlie."

It was Serena's turn to pose feet apart, hands on her hips. "That would be a very bad idea, Sheriff. You do something like that up in the mountains and you might never make it home."

"What is it with you people? You got no respect for the law. Well. For you information, Missy, we ain't in them mountains of yours at the moment so, you need to take yourself off on home. You just git, and let me talk with this man right here." Franklin turned back to Jesse. "Okay, I'm not saying I believe you, but if it wasn't you that found the body, who did?"

"I can't be sure, naturally, but I believe it was Big Tom."

"Tom McAdoo? He's a moonshiner."

"Is he? I had no idea."

"You damned well do too know he is. Where will I find him?"

"Who? Big Tom? Up on the mountain I expect."

"Up on the…Are you going to tell me how to find him or do I have to introduce you to the rubber hose we keep at the station to persuade you hillbillies to talk?"

Jesse felt his face redden and for a split second calculated the move he would need to make to put this big oaf on the ground. He took a breath. "Well, sir, if he is a moonshiner like you say, you won't never find him. If he ain't, well you drive up that dirt road over there, take the first fork to the right, Drive a mite more past three more forks, keeping to the right on them, and take the next one to the left. That'll get you there, alright. But, Sheriff, I think, if I was you, I'd drive real slow and tap your horn button when you get close to make sure he knows you're coming. We're not used to having the Law up on the mountain, you know. Fact is, you all don't ever come up, not even for a social. So, tap your horn and keep your hands where he can see them. He's a mite touchy, you could say."

Franklin took a step forward and dropped his hand to the butt of his pistol. Jesse shifted his weight to the balls of his feet and looked for a tell. Did this man lead with his right or was he a bull rusher? Would he pull that .38 caliber police special and use it as a club? R.G. wheeled around the corner.

"What the hell are you doing, Dalton? This man is my foreman and a war hero, to boot. What were you thinking? We all know what happens at that station of yours. Well, you are not going to put a book on my foreman's head and pound it with your damned club. You got that?"

"I got a duty to perform, R.G."

"And I got a business to run and if you have any hope of being elected to the job permanent next fall, you will let me get on with it."

"What is with you damned hill people?"

Jesse shrugged. "It's probably all that intermarriage you talked about. Having three eyes and pointy heads makes us suspicious of normal people."

The sheriff spun around and stalked off with a dismissive wave over his shoulder. "We aren't done here, boy. I'll be back."

"I'll be right here, Sheriff. Did I mention we got us a pig? We named him Dalton. Fat son of a bitch."

R.G. put a hand on Jesse's arm. "Take it easy, Jesse. You do not want that man against you."

"How'd he ever get himself elected in the first place?"

"Well, he wasn't elected, exactly. Sheriff Henry Spitz got the flu along with a slew of other folks and didn't make it. Franklin was pushed in as his deputy and then got himself appointed to fill the spot until Election Day."

"What slow cooker decided to appoint that loaf of stale bread sheriff?"

"Truth is, he joined up fairly recently. He worked at his uncle's ice house before that, but was let go. It's a bad day when your own kin don't keep you on. So then he got himself signed on as a deputy. He's married to the county superintendant's cousin, Bessie Sackmiller."

"Oh, Lordy, that's right. I forgot. Old Bouncing Bessie. No wonder he's hot under the collar."

"Who? You know her?"

"It was a nickname us boys give her. I couldn't have been more'n sixteen and we would…never mind. So, he married Bouncing Bessie. She must have got mad at him and said something."

"So, okay, I guess that intermarriage thing depends on who's married to whom, and you are grinning way too much, Jesse."

"Sorry about that. So, my cousin Anse is bearing false witness. I guess I ain't surprised. That boy has more meanness in him than a rattlesnake. If all this ain't enough to justify mountain mouthwash, nothing is." Jesse grinned and grabbed the packages out of the Ford's backseat. R.G. grabbed another.

"Serena is right," he said. That is one fine-looking hat you got yourself, Jesse."

"You run on up to Picketsville next week sometime and you can get yourself one just like it, or better. Only one thing, don't tell that peddler how much you got in your pocketbook. He'll find a way to relieve you of every last penny."

Chapter Fifteen

Work at the mill did not end until nearly seven o'clock. In October, that created new hazards. Sawing timber in daylight had enough potential risks for the workers. Doing it in failing light only added to them. Jesse said something to R.G. who only shrugged and reminded him that he had an order due the next day and there was only so much daylight available. Toward the end, Jesse pulled his Ford up to the track and trained its headlights on the spinning saw blade. He couldn't be sure if that helped very much, but the men all seemed to feel safer, even if they weren't. They'd risk losing a hand before they'd risk losing their jobs. R.G. was not a greedy man or a hard one. He was a product of hard times and these were hard times. His men didn't complain. It was what it was.

Jesse's watch read eight when he made the trip to the Spring House. Serena waited for him as she'd promised, but she did not appear pleased.

"You planning on spending the night, Jesse?" she said. Then she realized what she'd said could be taken another way. "Um, never mind that. I meant only that—"

"Exactly what did you mean, Miss Barker? I swear, you mountain women have no shame."

"You stop that talk right now, Jesse, or I will be away from here quicker than Halley's Comet."

"You was only nine when it come by. How'd you come to see it, back in the woods where you are?"

"You think you are so smart. We all climbed up to the top of the mountain and saw it clear as day. My Pa had read up on it and he said we might never see it again unless we lived clean to 1985."

"Okay, if you say so. I wasn't that lucky. Nobody in my family had a notion about comets, stars, or the ones that they say are not stars, but planets like the moon only they ain't. By the time the word made its way over to us, it were mostly gone. So, getting back to why we're here, I did that search like I said. I thought you could help me figure out what to do next."

"Well, if you had got here before the sun set, maybe I could have helped you, but there's only a little bitty crescent moon and I can't see the writing on that paper."

"If it were a full moon, you could. Look here I'll light a Lucifer and you can see enough to get the sense of it."

"I hope you have a whole box of strike-anywhere matches because this could take a while. Okay…" Serena squinted at the paper in the flickering light. The match burned down and Jesse lit another. Seven matches and a burned finger from the last one and Serena nodded. "I think I read it all. It's complicated, that's for sure."

"What does 'entailed' mean?"

"It's like the kings and dukes in Europe. Over there, the title and the castle, things like that, pass from oldest son to oldest son. The younger ones don't get anything when the old man dies."

"That don't seem fair."

"No, but Mister Conklin at the school said that was why most of us are here. Second sons and on down the line had nothing to do, no land, no money, nothing, so they joined the Army, took up pirating, or came to America. He said that most of us up in this part of the country could probably trace our family back to some old castle or something."

"That doesn't appeal much to me. I reckon a big castle might be better than a cabin with a dirt floor, but who would you spend your time with?"

"I don't expect that is a problem we need to worry about. Anyway, whoever it is that owns the land is a man and doesn't know he has title. We need to try and trace it somehow."

"What happens if there isn't an oldest son?"

"Then it goes to oldest male relative and so on."

"So, somebody who could be a second or third cousin to this man might own the land?"

"Yep. And here's the other thing, the name on this title is Leigh, Fairchild Leigh. That's pronounced, Lee, but spelled L-E-I-G-H. I guess that's where the stories about it being one of the Lees must have come from. On the other hand, people are always changing the way they spell their name, so we might have to check out Lees, Leighs, Leahs, and who knows what else."

"You're saying we should give up?"

"No, I'm saying it won't be easy. There is a better-than-even chance whoever owns this land is still local. We need to poke around and find someone with that name. It could even be a middle name or a maiden name."

"Now's when I wish Solomon was still alive. That boy could recite who was related to who like he had a map in his head. He knew everybody out to third and fourth cousins."

"Next best thing is Granny Fielder. She knows everything."

"She's crazy as a Betsy bug."

"She's your cousin, isn't she?"

"That one, I will let go. Listen, not everyone up here is really a cousin, you know. We are connected in lots of ways and not all of them is by blood."

"Well, you think on it for a while. I have to git. It's late and folks will be wondering what I'm up to and if they find out I spend some time up here in the woods in the dark with you, they might just insist on a wedding. I don't know about you, but I am definitely not ready for that step, Mister Jesse Sutherlin."

"What? You're not ready to get yoked to a man who has traveled Europe, has seen Paris, France, has exchanged serious, you could even say life or death, messages with gentlemen of several other countries, not to mention their lady friends. You would turn your back on all that?"

"Well when you put it that way, it's mighty tempting, but yep, turning my back."

"Then you'd better skedaddle. I think I hear someone coming."

Serena slipped away in the dark. Jesse cleared his throat and shuffled his feet. He wanted whomever was working their way up the hill to be drawn him and not hear Serena. She moved quietly, but mountain ears didn't miss much.

"Is that you, Jesse Sutherlin?"

Jesse did not recognize the voice. He slid off the log he'd been sitting on and stepped behind the trunk of a tree. If there was going to be shooting, he wanted some protection.

"Who's asking?"

"Albert Lebrun. I come to talk."

"What about?"

"Your cousin and who might have shot him. Where're you at?"

"I'm sitting on this here log right in front of you."

Lebrun moved into the clearing. The crescent moon barely lit the area, but there was just enough light for Jesse to see that he was alone and not armed. He stepped out from behind the tree and sat.

"What do you want to know?"

"I think it's more about what do you want to know, ain't it?"

"Point taken. Why are you talking to me?"

"You saved Jake Barker's life. That means that the word in the community that you are serious about catching the man who shot Solomon McAdoo is right. You aren't ready to start a shooting war with us. That right?"

"It is. What can you tell me?"

"Two things. One, it weren't any one of us that pulled the trigger. Two, whoever done it, ain't from over on our side of the mountain. It's possible that one of them might have seen something. I'm saying, might have. That help?"

"It ought to, but it don't. See, the folks over here are pretty hot. Just saying it weren't someone from you-all's side would be seen as a lie and enough to send them howling over there like a pack of bluetick coonhounds."

"That's not good."

"No, it ain't."

"What are you going to do?"

"Ask a favor. Can you keep your ear to the ground? Somebody knows something and will talk sooner or later. You said that someone over on your side might have seen something. Find me that witnesses if that part is true. I know there were two people up at that still that either saw what happened or were party to it. At least one of them will hint at knowing something soon enough. It's just human nature to allow as how you're knowing an important secret. If you hear anything, anything at all, you tell Serena Barker and she will tell me."

"I can do that." They say quietly for a minute. "You're working down at the sawmill, they say."

"Yep."

"Is there any openings? I know a thing or two about sawmills."

"You'd better check with Mister R.G. Anderson. You were in France, too, weren't you, Albert?"

"Yeah, I joined up right after you. Spent my time tending to them newfangled tank machines, though. Mostly being a grease monkey, you know? I didn't get near enough to the front to see any action. Not like you, anyway."

"Count your blessings, Albert. It weren't no picnic. Anyway, Old R.G. fancies ex-soldiers and we just got ourselves some Allis Chalmers tractors. I reckon we might could use somebody who can turn a wrench and knows his way around a gas motor. If there is an opening, you'd get first go at it."

"Thanks for the tip. I better go 'fore someone finds me consorting with the enemy. Oh, and for the record, we never met."

"Never saw you. Good luck. I'll be waiting for news."

Albert disappeared into the forest. Jesse took three steps to his right and ducked back behind his tree. He scooped up a handful of pebbles and tossed them, one at a time into the woods. He sent each one a bit farther down the path. For anyone waiting in the dark and listening, Jesse was on his way down the hill.

A minute passed. Jesse breathed as lightly as he could. The air seemed to have become thick and the darkness, which had never bothered him before, now felt menacing. Jesse started to step away when he heard them. Then he saw them, three men separated from the forest and stepped quietly into the clearing next to the Spring House. He heard the soft murmur of voices. He could not make out what they discussed or who they were. Their words were muffled, their voices indistinct. Did he recognize a voice? He could not say. They pivoted and looked first in the direction they must have believed Jesse had taken, then the other way. He waited.

A decision made, the three men trailed off after Albert, leaving as quietly as they had come. Were they Albert's backup if things had gone wrong? Had Albert worried that if he met with a McAdoo, he'd be bushwhacked? Or were these three following Albert for some other reason? Jesse decided he wouldn't risk going after them to find out.

Chapter Sixteen

Jesse worked his way home in the dark. He didn't notice or hear anything out of the ordinary on the way. Night music, they called it on Buffalo Mountain. That would be owls hooting, tree frogs peeping, an occasional hound belling for whatever reason only it knew, and crickets. The air had become chilled, announcing winter couldn't be too far away. Jesse thought he'd start bringing home slabs and wood scraps. It would beat chopping firewood and he hadn't noticed any stack near the house anyway. He'd need to have a word with Abel about that. He saw the lantern as he turned in off the road.

Addie Sutherlin rocked on the front porch. A single lantern burned on the chair next to hers. Its wick had been trimmed back and the light it gave off barely illuminated her face. She rocked forward as Jesse's boot hit the first step.

"Where you been, Son? Can't you see it's dark? Here I am worrying about you and burning perfectly good kerosene for no good reason."

"I'll buy you some more."

"It's a nickel a quart now. You got so much money you can throw it away like that?"

"I am sorry, Ma. You didn't have to wait up for me, you know. I am all grown up now."

"You say so, but here it is way past the time normal folks are getting their sleep and you are gallivanting all over the mountain.

Abel says you're sparking that Barker girl. You stay away from her, you hear?"

"Now why should I do that?"

"She's from the other side of the mountain. Ain't no good—"

"First off, we been over this once already and, number two, I ain't sparking anybody at the moment."

"Then what were you doing?"

"Checking on a few things is all. I had to meet somebody."

"In the dark?"

"Sometimes that's when you have to do things, Ma. Dark can cover a lot of bad but it also can help with a heap of good. Stop worrying about me. Listen, before you set off on another one of your journeys with advice, country wisdom, and dire warnings, I need some information that maybe you can give me. Do you know, or have you ever heard of a Fairchild Leigh? I believe that is how you pronounce his name only it is spelled funny like 'light' only with no T at the end and an extra E in there, so maybe it's Lee-ig, Lie-egg. Lee is what Sara said it's pronounced as, though, and she's had some serious schooling."

"You can't trust what them Lebruns say."

"I told you. She isn't one of them and besides, I think I'd trust her a whole lot farther than I would Anse McAdoo and his family any day."

"Well, I'm just saying."

"I hear you. Fairchild Leigh?"

"Well, I know of him, Jesse. It would be back a spell. Your grandpa would have known him, probably. Yes, he was a figure most folks had a peek at one way or the other."

"How?"

"This would be after the war, you understand. I'm talking about the war we fought against the Yankees."

"The Civil War."

"The War of Northern Aggression. Come on, Jesse, have you forgot everything you learned in school?"

"About that war, maybe I have. Go on, tell me about Leigh."

"Fairchild Lee, however you spell it, led a band of night riders."

"What?"

"Those were hard times, Jesse. The War, Mister Lincoln's War, and Reconstruction that came after it, created a hardship for most folks who happened to have chose the losing side. They called them carpetbaggers, only in this part of the world they were more like pickpockets that came down the valley stealing folks' land and their onlyist belongings. Well, Fairchild put together a group of men, they say there was like to sixty, but your grandpa said it were more like fifteen or twenty. They'd ride up and down the valley and settle with the Yankees who came down here and sucked up land that weren't theirs that fell to tax default. See, if you can't work because you were on the losing side, you can't very well pay your taxes."

"Soldiers couldn't work after the war? Well, some things don't change."

"There you are. Well, you look at poor Bobby Lee. He lost his estate up there in Arlington to them Yankees and the only job he could get was being the head of some dinky little college in Lexington next to Stonewall Jackson's old school. Anyway, that situation got corrected after a bit, but not before a whole lot of acreage changed hands. Fairchild Leigh, he made it hard on them that took advantage of them folks and chased a good number back to wherever they came from."

"What happened to him?"

"Well, sir, nobody knows for a certainty. Story was he bought himself a commission and went off to fight the Bonaparte French in Mexico. They say he never came home from that."

"Did he have a wife, a family?"

"Don't think so. Not at the end, anyway. Some say his wife and children were killed in one of the raids Sheridan made down this way. I don't know if that's true, though. They say that's why he was so angry at the Yankees who come down here after. He might have had a brother or sister. Wait, that was it. A sister. He had this sister who married and went west, I think."

"So there'd be nieces and nephews?"

"I suppose so. Why do you want to know?"

"Because one of them owns the Spring House property and I'd like to talk with them about buying the timber rights."

"What? What are you doing fooling around with things like that?

"Trying not to be a stupid hillbilly, Ma. There's way too much of that going around."

"What are you talking about?"

"Getting ahead. This land is played out. You know that. Pa knew that. Short of making moonshine and working in the timber business two hours traveling time away, there ain't a whole lot of opportunities around here. Big timbering is pretty much dead and gone from this mountain, but R.G. Anderson has a specialty wood business. He hired me on and that's what I got. It's what I will work with 'til something better comes along. Buying and selling timber rights could make me some real money."

"Land, you sound like your Pa, bless his soul. Always talking about a payday, getting off the mountain, building a proper house. Well, that never came about, did it?"

"Influenza got him, Ma. If it hadn't, who knows, he might have made it."

"Influenza killed a lot more than just folks, I reckon."

"It did. You remember a name for this sister of Fairchild Leigh?"

"Maybe, if I think on it for a while. So, what you going to do with a lot of money?"

"I told you. I'm getting you one of them iceboxes."

"Pshaw. That there is pure foolishness…MacElvaine."

"What?"

"MacElvaine was her married name. Fairchild Leigh's sister. She married a MacElvaine and went to Cincinnati or someplace out there in Ohio. Or maybe it was Cleveland. There ain't much difference in places once you get past the mountains, they tell me."

"Well, now, that is definitely not true, Ma. Every place has its own personality, like."

"Land sakes, you has got to be a know-it-all since you went away. You don't hear Abel back-talking to me."

"It ain't back talk, Ma. I speak truth in love."

"What in all that's holy does that mean?"

"It's what people say after they insult you, your family, everything you believe in, and they think it makes their rude-ness okay, I guess."

"Horse feathers! I'm off to bed and you should be, too."

"In a minute. I need to have a time to think some things through."

Chapter Seventeen

The next morning Jesse awoke to find the day had started out with a cold, bone-chilling, misty rain that made it clear that winter had crept closer than he'd figured. Worse, the weather did not match up with anything Jesse had to wear. His stint in the Army and the natural process of growing up had left him with few coats in the chifforobe he could wear now. At least none he could wear without popping a seam. He considered wearing his uniform greatcoat. It was woolen, after all, but decided against it. Too many dark memories that went with that garment. He found an old blanket coat that his father had worn back when he was bigger and it fit reasonably well. While the weather caused him to struggle with what to wear, it suited his dark mood. He only had two days left on Big Tom's deadline. Except an assurance from Albert Lebrun that none of his clan had pulled the trigger, he had come up with nothing new regarding Solomon's murder. More importantly, he had "The Feeling."

In the trenches, men would become morose, or frightened, or panicked. There did not seem to be any cause, any reason, any sense to it, beyond a conviction in impending doom. "The Feeling" had to do with the certainty that they would be dead by nightfall. Everyone who slogged across France and sat in a trench took it as a matter of fact that they would not go home alive, that their destiny was to spend eternity under six feet of French dirt. For them, it wasn't a matter of *if*, but *when*. So, the day you got "The Feeling," you knew that it would be your last day on Earth. Whether that led to carelessness, or recklessness on their part, or some other cosmic force came into play, no one knew, but many of those who experienced it did, indeed, die within the ensuing twenty-four hours. And so, on this rainy, cold morning, Jesse knew for an absolute certainty that something bad would happen before the sun dropped over the mountain to the west. He shivered and the chill in the air played only a small part in that. He stepped out into the icy drizzle and cranked his Model T. Good day or bad, he had a job to do.

He arrived before his gang showed up to start the big saw blades whirring. He took the opportunity to step into the office in hopes of finding Serena. He wanted to tell her what he'd learned about Fairchild Leigh. Before he could say anything, she held up her hand, palm forward.

"Jesse, did you have anything to do with Albert Lebrun last night?"

"Last night? No. Why?"

"He's missing and he told his Pa he might be meeting up with one of the McAdoos. The only McAddo I could think of who that could be, was you. So, no Albert?"

Jesse considered taking Serena into his confidence. After all, she had been party to what he hoped to accomplish from the very beginning. But, he'd promised Albert he wouldn't say anything and for the moment he would keep that promise.

"Nope. Now let me tell you what I found out about Leigh."

"You can tell me at lunch. It's time you blew the whistle."

Jesse checked his watch. It was. He hurried out to the yard and, noting there was enough steam in the large rig, yanked the lanyard. The whistle sounded, a sliver of sun fought its way through the clouds, and the day began.

• • ● • •

The noon whistle blew and the men relaxed from their work. The pulleys were disengaged and the belts that drove the equipment lurched to a halt. Jesse pulled off his work gloves and slapped them against his knee. He dusted his hat and picked up his coat which he had removed as he warmed to the work. R.G. stepped out of the office and waved to him. Jesse nodded and started toward the office. He thought he saw Serena in a window gesticulating. The expression on her face was anything but happy. He paused and tried to read her lips. Was she saying "run"?

He rounded the corner of the building and felt someone grab his wrist and try to force him face-forward against the wall. He didn't think. He seized the wrist that held him twisted it backwards and yanked. Sheriff Dalton P. Franklin dropped to his knees with a howl and tried, unsuccessfully, to draw his service revolver.

"By goddamn I got you for resisting arrest, you stump-jumper. Suspicion of murder and resisting arrest. You're cooked, boy."

Jesse pushed the sheriff off, but took three steps back and shifted his weight forward. "I don't know a whole lot about the law, Sheriff, but I think you have to announce that you plan to arrest someone before you can say he was resisting it. All I know is you ambushed me. You didn't say anything about arresting me or anybody else."

Dalton Franklin struggled to get his bulk upright, the effort made more difficult because he tried to undo the snap on his holster at the same time. "I did. You're just thick in the head like all you people, and the judge is going to hear that."

"You pull the pistol out one inch and I will personally break your arm, Sheriff. You want to arrest me, you go ahead, but you be thinking careful how you go about it. This time say the words."

"Listen, boy, you ain't in no position to threaten me. If I say I said it, I did and that's the official version."

R.G. Anderson appeared at the sheriff's shoulder. "No you didn't, Dalton. Jesse's right. You jumped him before he could even see you. I am a witness to that. I can also swear there ain't a mark on this boy so at this moment, if he shows up at his arraignment with so much as a broke fingernail, I'll have you for lunch. Now, who was murdered and why is Jesse a suspect?"

"That, as you very well know, Anderson, is strictly police business and I am not at liberty to say."

"Well, Sheriff, if you are planning on putting my foreman in handcuffs, you have to say why and that would include the name of the alleged victim, ain't that right?"

"Sum bitch, when did you get to be a lawyer? I don't have to do any such a thing."

"Trust me when I tell you, yes you do. Shall I call Judge Watkins and ask for a legal opinion?"

The sheriff fumed and rubbed his wrist. He glared at R.G. and then at Jesse. He did not like being told how to do his job. He stuck out his chest and hitched up his pants. To his apparent dismay, all the glaring and puffing changed nothing. R.G. did not back down.

"Okay, then. Jesse Sutherlin, I am arresting you on a charge of suspicion of murder in that you stabbed Albert Lebrun to death sometime last night. Before you say anything, I have a witness that puts the two of you together up on the mountain at a place referred to as 'The Spring House.' Now, turn around and gimme your wrists."

"That witness wouldn't be named Hansel again, would it? No, this time it's Gretel. As much as you want me to be the murderer, you got the wrong man, Sheriff."

"Oh, I don't think so. You thought you were being so smart yesterday. Well, who's the smart one now?"

Franklin shoved Jesse in the general direction of his automobile.

"Don't you worry about a thing, Jesse," R.G. said. "I'll be down this afternoon with the best lawyer in the county." He spun on his heel and headed for the office. "Don't forget what I said, Dalton—not even a broken nail."

Franklin pretended not to hear and shoved Jesse to his car. "One peep out of you, bucko, and your employer looking out for you or not, I will introduce you to Billy." He tapped the baton in his belt.

"That would be a very bad idea, Sheriff."

"That's the ticket. You just keep on running your mouth, sonny-boy. It's what just makes tossing saps like you in the pokey so much fun. Now shut your trap and get in the car."

Chapter Eighteen

"On your feet, mountain boy. Your lawyer's here."

Jesse struggled to right himself. He'd been stretched out on the cell cot, nursing his eye and aching head. His breakfast of cornmeal mush in its cracked bowl remained on the floor. Mice had eaten about half before Jesse even knew it had been shoved through the slot in the door. The jailer slid in a key and the door clanked open. A man in a shiny suit and red necktie stepped in.

"Nicholas Bradford, Esquire," he said. "Your employer, R.G. Anderson, has engaged me to represent you. I have petitioned Judge Watkins to move quickly on this because I am convinced the sheriff has no case beyond hearsay. On the other hand, R.G. believes if you are kept here long enough he, that is to say the sheriff, will find the means, or more accurately, will find a stooge, to build a more substantial one. That could be very bad for you. Now, tell me exactly what in Billy Blue Blazes is going on here."

Jesse filled him in on Solomon's death, his attempts to solve the murder or at least defuse the tension between the rival families on the mountain. He recounted the conversation he'd had with Albert Lebrun and what he'd told him. Bradford sat on the edge of the cot and jotted notes in a small leatherbound book with a filigreed gold mechanical pencil. He asked questions and made Jesse clarify a few points.

"So, to review, you met this Albert Lebrun two nights ago. You had a conversation regarding the shooting of a cousin of yours, Solomon McAdoo. Albert told you in no uncertain terms that no one of his acquaintance, that is to say his immediate or extended family, had anything to do with the shooting. Is that about it?"

Jesse frowned, which made his eye hurt which, in turn, caused him to wince.

"Hmmm. What happened to your eye?"

"I tripped and fell on the sheriff's fist."

"I see. Did he also introduce you to his encyclopedia?"

"Pardon?"

"The sheriff is known for helping his interrogations along by putting a book, usually a volume of the Britannica, on a prisoner's head and whacking the book with his truncheon. Were you entertained in that manner?"

Jesse grinned. "Well, yes. He put that book right on my head and tried to pound some knowledge into me. It was very educational."

"It was? In what way?"

"I learned a trick or two about holding a conversation with Sheriff Franklin and propose to return the favor the next time he drops in for a visit."

"That I would like to see. So, back to the narrative. Have I got the essentials?"

"All except the part about the three men who followed Albert after he left me."

"Three men?"

"Well, before I walked down the path, see, I chucked some stones down it first. If anyone were listening in the dark, they'd figure I was off and away. A minute later three men stepped out of the woods and sort of had a pow-wow and then disappeared in the same direction Albert took. I'm pretty sure those three men were following him."

"But you can't say with certitude they did?"

"If that means did I know for sure they did, no, sir. Why is that important?"

"It's important, Jesse, because if you said you knew absolutely, it begs the question, 'How do you know?' It means you had to have followed them, and the prosecutor, if we get that far, which

I aim to see we don't, could speculate you were in position to stab Albert after all, you see?"

"I'll need to ponder that one, Mister Bradford. Is there anything else?"

Tell me about the war, your war."

"The war? I can't see what that has to do with this."

"Trust me."

"Well, shoot, there ain't much to tell, Counselor. It was long days of sitting in the mud scratching lice and being bored to death followed by short days of noise, being scared out of your wits, shooting, fighting, blood, people next to you dying, and not knowing what was going on. Then, back to scratching and being bored. That's pretty much it."

"That's not what I hear. You received a medal, right? Okay, what about your cousin who was killed?"

"Solomon? Most folks would say he wasn't anything special. Me and him served together in the war. Solomon didn't fare too well, though. Shell shock got him."

"That happened to a lot of men, didn't it?"

"I hear so, yes. In my company, which is all I know about, we had near a dozen go that way. We were hit pretty hard out there, with the shelling and all. Other units got off a little easier, I guess, and didn't have the problem so bad."

"But Solomon, he made it home and was functioning?"

"Functioning? Sorry…?"

"Able to work, eat, you know, fit in."

"I don't know about fitting in. He did his chores and pitched in alright, but he got harassed a whole lot by the young folk and some of the meaner older ones who'd make a loud noise when he weren't looking—you know, like bang a stick on the table or maybe shoot off their gun, and he go to pieces. Some thought that were funny."

"You?"

"It weren't funny and nobody did it if I was around or, if they did, they experienced some close acquaintance with my knuckles."

"Okay. Judge Watkins says he'll hold a preliminary hearing at two. If the sheriff hasn't done any better in the way of evidence by then, you'll be home in time for your supper. In the meantime, get some rest and try not to provoke the sheriff or his men."

"Provoke?"

"You didn't get that shiner from being a cooperative witness, did you? I'll see you at two. I have a passel of telephone calls to make."

"Yes, sir. Excuse me, but—"

"There's something else?"

"It doesn't have a thing to do with this, but...well, I looked up this title to a piece of land and I want to find out who the descendents of the owner were."

"What? Son, you are being fitted up for a noose and you're worried about a piece of land?"

"It's that bad? If I understand Sheriff Franklin's 'evidence' aright, he's got the word of someone who says they saw me with Albert and I was the last one to do that. But that ain't true. There's them three others I told you about."

Bradford sat down again and studied Jesse. "Okay, listen to me. You saying there were three or a hundred and three people following Albert Lebrun doesn't mean diddly-squat unless one of them steps up and says, 'I was one of them.' What do you think the chances are that will happen? Don't you realize that if you are correct about the three men, one of them is most likely the person who killed Albert?"

"Oh." Jesse shook his head and stared at the floor. "Mister Bradford, it seems like I might have recognized one of the voices, maybe. It wasn't like I knew it straight off, but more like it was familiar somehow. If that's so, it might have been a McAdoo. When I say something in court, they will step up and I'm in the clear, right?"

"Son, you better hope that voice wasn't a McAdoo. As nearly as I can determine, you don't have any friends on either side of the mountain."

"What? Mister Bradford, we're family, thick or thin."

"Really? Well, I've seen the deposition the sheriff has and I am not convinced."

Chapter Nineteen

Jesse had never been to court before, a fact which had to be counted as an oddity in as much as most of his adult relatives, given the nature of their alternative avocation and penchant for Saturday night brawls, had made their pilgrimage to the building at one time or another. Mountain life carried with it certain legal risks, you could say, chiefly difficulties with tax stamps required for selling consumable alcohol before, and now, with Prohibition, just the making of it. But somehow, Jesse had avoided all that. His lawyer, on the other hand, had all the experience either of them needed.

"Jesse, this is only a hearing, not a trial. The rules of evidence do not strictly apply. The sheriff, for reasons I cannot fathom, wants you behind bars with no possibility of bail. When the judge asks you a question, you stand up before you answer. You only answer questions if they are directed to you. Otherwise, you don't say anything. You are mute, got it?"

"I dummy up."

"Correct. You let me do the talking and, for heaven's sake, don't let the county attorney or the sheriff goad you into saying or doing something they can use against you later."

• • ● • •

Jesse was surprised at the number of people who showed up. He expected R.G. and some relatives. He imagined there'd be some Lebruns, naturally, and he hoped Serena would be there. She was, along with most of the McAdoos and Lebruns. The two camps sat on either side of the courtroom like families at a wedding and glared at each other. The balcony, ordinarily reserved for the colored community, had been usurped by Buffalo Mountain people as well.

The bailiff had made them all leave their guns outside so the threat of eminent war had been put on hold. The talking, most of it intentionally loud so as to be easily heard by everyone on the other side, soon turned into a dull roar. The clerk had to shout. "All rise," three times before everyone hushed and stood. A little man with a bald head and almost overwhelmed by black robes popped in through a side door. The bailiff added, "The Honorable Horace C. Watkins, presiding."

Judge Watkins took the bench, perched a pince-nez on his nose, adjusted his mustache with a forefinger, and rapped his gavel. The people sat. The clerk stood and sing-songed a charge sheet which mostly said, after the technical language was ignored, that an eyewitness had given the sheriff a signed statement attesting to the fact that Jesse Sutherlin was in the company of Albert Lebrun on that night and this same witness was prepared to offer evidence that the same Jesse Sutherlin was the last to see Albert alive. Moreover, it alleged the strong possibility he could be party to the murder of Albert Lebrun as everybody knew of the enmity between the two families and everybody knew that one of the same Jesse Sutherlin's cousins had been brutally slain some days before and, further, that he had vowed to find the murderer of his cousin.

Bradford stood. "Objection."

"What is the nature of your objection, Counselor?"

"Your Honor, these charges are capricious and pure hearsay."

"Overruled. For the record, you are?"

"Nicholas Bradford, counsel for Mister Sutherlin, the accused."

"Thank you. County Attorney Bowers, are you ready to present the County's case?"

"Yes, Your Honor, I am. The County holds that the accused, Jesse Sutherlin, is at the least, a material witness to and the possible perpetrator of the murder by stabbing of Albert Lebrun two nights ago. It is well known he was seeking the murderer of his cousin three days previously and had promised to bring that man to justice. It appears he thinks he did. We believe, given the history of enmity between the several families on Buffalo Mountain and the reputation each has for exhibiting little respect for the law, he should be considered a flight risk and we request he be detained in prison until such time as a trial can be scheduled."

"I see. Well, that is a big assumption. Just what do you have?"

"With the court's permission, I would like to interview Sheriff Dalton Franklin."

Bradford was back on his feet. "Stipulation, Your Honor."

"Which is?"

"The sheriff be placed under oath."

"You don't think the sheriff will tell the truth?"

"We have concerns."

"So ordered. You may interview the sheriff under the stipulation just agreed to."

"Your Honor, the sheriff is hardly to be considered an unreliable—"

"As stipulated. Proceed."

The sheriff was sworn in. He did not look happy. He glared at Jesse and then at Bradford. Several McAdoos began to hoot. That in turn caused the Lebruns to respond in kind.

"Order, order. If there is any more unruliness, I will clear this courtroom and anyone slow to respond will, themselves, find accommodations in our jail. Proceed, Mister Bowers."

"Sheriff Franklin, you have persuasive evidence that the man sitting over there," he pointed at Jesse, "is complicit in the murder of one Albert Lebrun, is that not so?"

"Yes, sir. That boy is up to his ass...pardon...elbows in it, for sure."

"You consider him a flight risk?"

"You know as well as I do, them stump-jumpers is a thick as thieves. You turn that boy loose on the mountain and you'll never see him again, no sir."

Judge Watkins tapped his gavel. "What did you call the people?"

"Your Honor?"

"You just labeled a large number of voting constituents 'stump-jumpers.' Did I hear you right?"

"Well, Judge, you know how it is."

"I do. I've heard enough. Mr. Bradford, do you have anything to add?"

"Yes, Your Honor, Jesse Sutherlin admits to seeing Albert Lebrun the night of his murder. He met the deceased and had a conversation about an earlier murder which promised to start an internecine war on the mountain if it were not resolved speedily. They agreed to work together to do just that. Someone other than my client apparently did not want that to happen. That is, of course, only a supposition. Now, as to my client, Your Honor, he is not a flight risk. This charge is one hundred percent hearsay. We are presented with a witness statement that only places my client in the presence of the deceased. It *alleges* more, but proves nothing. Your Honor, my client is a steady working man. His employer trusts him with the operation of his mill. Furthermore, he is a genuine and decorated war hero. I will not go into the details, but I just got off the telephone with the War Office. This man here, received the Distinguished Service Cross for bravery and gallantry in the face of the enemy. He was promoted to Brevet Second Lieutenant, a battlefield commission, no mean achievement in itself. Well, Your Honor, we should be holding a parade for him, not tarring his name with this slanderous set of accusations."

"Your oratory is well known, Counselor. Thank you. Sheriff, what have you for me?"

"Well, Your Honor, we have a written and, by gum, signed statement that this man was the last to see the dead...the deceased alive. We have every reason to believe he's the one what done Albert in and he needs to be in the lockup."

"That's it? That's your case?"

"Well, yes, sir."

"Have a seat." The judge asked Jesse to stand. "Mister Sutherlin, you have anything to add?"

"No, sir. Except to say I most definitely was not the last to see Albert alive."

"You concede that you were with Albert Lebrun two nights ago but are suggesting there were others?"

"Yes, sir. After we ended our conversation and I slipped away, three men come out of the woods like they were maybe following Albert, and they took off after him."

"And he left your presence in one piece, you could say, and in the company of, or nearly so, of three other men?"

"Yes, Your Honor."

"Hmmm. Another thing, you have a black eye, Mister Sutherlin. I am reliably informed you did not have it when you were arrested. Is that correct?"

"Yes, sir, that is correct. No, sir, I didn't."

"Were you introduced to the sheriff's set of encyclopedias?"

The sheriff leaped to his feet. "Now, just a minute here, Judge. This man was resisting arrest. He was a clear threat to the safety of my officers and this line of questioning's got nothing to do with the case."

"Sit down, Dalton. I asked the accused a question. Mister Sutherlin, the encyclopedia?"

Jesse only smiled and shrugged.

Judge Watkins sat back and stroked his mustache for a moment. "As near as I can see, Sheriff, you have nothing. Mister Sutherlin, you are free to go." The judge banged his gavel and stood to leave.

The sheriff jumped to his feet and shook his fist in the general direction of the bench. "There's an election coming, Judge. You might want to think twice about how you disrespect police work in your court."

Judge Watkins, turned toward Sheriff Franklin, a thin smile on his face. "Dalton, I could say the same to you. This court's adjourned."

Chapter Twenty

Jesse made his way through the crowd of friends and relatives. He caught Serena's eye. She risked a smile in spite of the press of Lebruns around her. He nodded. He'd find a way to talk to her later. McAdoos in name or connected by marriage pounded him on the back while dozens of angry Lebrun eyes followed him out the door.

"Well, that's settled, then," Big Tom declared. "I didn't think you'd get her done, Jesse. I swear, I thought you talking all peaceable like, we wouldn't get us Solomon's shooter in a year, much less four days."

"What? Wait, Grandpa, you think I killed Albert Lebrun?"

"Well, sure you did, didn't you? Hell, it don't matter a flea's rear end if it was you or Abel. It's done and there's an end to it."

"I didn't and he didn't and Albert didn't kill Solomon. Grandpa, this isn't an end. Jumping Jehoshaphat, this is a beginning."

As if on cue, John Henry Lebrun shoved his way through the crowd and stood in front of Jesse.

"You think you got away with murder, but you ain't, Jesse Sutherlin. You think you killed Albert and evened the score? Well, you didn't and I reckon there's a price to pay and you'll be the one to pay it. You and your family need to watch out."

"John Henry, whatever you heard, it ain't true. I did not stab your cousin. We met and together were aiming to work out who shot Solomon. He was fixing to join me working at the mill, for Lord's sake."

"Albert? Working at the sawmill? Don't make me laugh. Albert were a mountain man through and through. We cut timber, we make likker, we don't work for no flatlander."

"You're wrong about that, too. Solomon McAdoo is dead and who killed him is still a mystery. Albert Lebrun is dead and whoever stabbed him is a mystery, too, and I ain't got the foggiest notion who did either of them things, but it's clear as day I'm wasting my time talking to you all."

John Henry turned to the crowd. "You all listen to me, you McAdoos. I ain't looking to start no feud, but I ain't letting this killing go either. So, here's what I aim to do." He spun back to Jesse. "You and me, Jesse Sutherlin, three days from now over at the Spring House. Just the two of us. You stabbed Albert, so we will have it out with knives. Whoever wins, well that settles it once and for all."

Lebrun pushed his way out and walked away.

Big Tom scratched his head and looked Jesse in the eye. "Now what in hell was that all about?"

"What that was all about was there ain't no end to this. Albert Lebrun didn't kill Solomon. I didn't kill Albert, so instead of one murder to figure out to stop you all from starting a shooting war, now I got two. Top that off with John Henry Lebrun aiming to carve me up. You have any suggestions for me about what I have to do next?"

"You ain't going to that Spring House alone, Jesse. We will be there and if they try anything funny, we'll fix them good."

"You haven't heard a word I've said. Will somebody help me out here?"

Twenty pairs of blank McAdoo eyes stared at him. Jesse turned on his heel and strode away.

"Now where in the dickens are you off to?"

"Grandpa, I'm off to see if there is one not-crazy person left in the county, that's where."

• • ● • •

Serena found him sitting on a fallen tree trunk down the hill from the now infamous Spring House.

"Why'd you tell me you didn't see Albert when you did?"

"I'm sorry about that, Serena."

"It's because I'm a Lebrun?"

"What? No. I gave my word to Albert, that's all. When you asked me, I didn't know he was dead."

"Would you have told me, if you had?"

"I hope so. I ain't too good with maybe questions, Serena."

"So, what will you do? Will you fight John Henry? Over on my side of the mountain, he's reckoned as the best knife-fighter anywhere. He'll kill you, Jesse."

"I ain't decided. What do you think I should do?"

"You're asking me? You trust the judgment of a woman?"

"Now don't you go getting all suffragette on me. 'Course I do. You might be the only set of brains in working order on this here mountain."

"Well, I'll take that as a compliment, thank you. All right then, I will give you my advice, but I'm betting you won't take it. You need to go away, Jesse. Pack up your 'Old Kit Bag' and smile or no smile, head north, south, east, or west, it don't matter which. Just go. This is a fight you can't win. The two clans have been itching for an excuse to start shooting. Solomon, Albert, alive or dead, sooner or later, something was going to set them off and that's a fact. The only end I see to all this is a passel of dead folk. Newspapers crowing about backwoods justice and ignorant mountain folk and right there in the middle of it is Jesse Sutherlin. And guess what? The deadest of them all is going to be you. Pack a bag and get out."

"I should just turn tail and run?"

"Don't even start that. You're better'n that, Jesse."

"You're right. I got nothing to prove in that department. Okay, I will go on one condition."

"What's that?"

"That you go with me."

"Me? Whatever put that notion in your head? I can't leave. Well, I could, but not now, and not with you."

"Why not now? Why not with me?"

Serena leaned toward Jesse and looked in his eyes. "I ain't ready for that kind of commitment, Jess."

"Not ready to commit to leaving or not ready to admitting that we have moved some this last week and it makes sense to keep moving?"

"Stop."

"Well. That's my condition. I ain't running alone and that's the hard truth. I'll only run if you run with me. Since it appears you ain't up for that, I guess I'll have to stay and work this problem out on my own."

"Jesse, you're impossible. How you ever convinced those people to make you an officer, I'll never understand. Do they give extra points for pigheadedness?"

"No, more like for stupid."

Serena gazed at him for another minute and sighed. "You're awful. What's a brevet?"

"A what?"

"Lawyer Bradford said in court you were a Brevet Lieutenant. I heard of First and Second Lieutenants. Never heard of Brevet. What's that?"

"Oh. Well, it means temporary, sort of. It means that when the war ended, unless someone said otherwise, I would be set back to my real rank, which by then was Corporal. Only it didn't happen. It could have, but it didn't."

"Because?"

"They needed volunteers, particularly officers, to go fight the Bolsheviks in Russia. They made my promotion permanent when I said I might be interested."

"But you didn't go."

"No. I changed my mind and they were way too busy to bother with fixing the paperwork. Then we all come home and it didn't make a difference."

Serena sighed and stood. "You're going to do what you're going to do, Jesse. I will worry about you now and cry at your funeral later. Why must you be so stubborn?"

She wheeled and ran down the mountain.

"Born that way, I guess. Well, shoot, you don't have to run off like that…" He watched her disappear into the trees. "Good talking to you, Serena."

Jesse picked up a stick and began scratching the dirt at his feet with it.

Chapter Twenty-one

The next day was Sunday. Jesse knew he would not be getting a thing done today. If he asked a question, he'd get a blank stare for an answer. Nothing except the necessary would be done today. Cows would be milked, chickens and pigs fed, fires lit, and some cooking done for those with food enough to require it. But it was the Lord's day and that meant a day spent in church listening to Preacher Primrose and the other Deacons rail on about the wages of sin, the scarlet women who had led good, God-fearing boys astray, fornication, raucous living, all accompanied by multiple references to Hell, fire, and brimstone. The Bible, which two of them had never read, they being functionally illiterate, was quoted often in verses selected to reinforce their rolling sermons and punctuated with "ahs" when they needed to catch a breath. Men and women moved in and out of the building, to have a smoke, spread a picnic, or just to pass the time. One or two of the men would slip behind the church for a pull on a jar, jug, or bottle. After a bit, they'd wander back in or go on home. The constant ebb and flow of congregants had no effect whatever on the preachers or their oratory which went on uninterrupted. Since France, Jesse reckoned he'd already been to Hell and it weren't anything like as bad as the preachers said.

Like most everybody else on the mountain, Lebrun or McAdoo, he'd put on his best clothes, scraped the whiskers off his face with the Gillette safety razor that had been given to him by the Army, and set out. Dressed and his suit brushed, he'd make his way to the little church down the mountain from his place. When he was still a shirttail kid, he'd sneak away, unimpressed by the threat of Devil's imps which he's been told lurked around every corner and tree. Instead, he and Abel, when he got bigger, and some of the braver cousins would gather chestnuts, smoke some purloined tobacco, or simply loaf under a tree, freed for one day of chores and school.

The funny thing about Sunday church was that both McAdoo and Lebrun folks sat together in the same pews. They intoned together "Rock of Ages," "A Closer Walk With Thee," or any of the dozen old standards sung in that church over the years. One or two even would manage a harmony-like line on top, which the organ player, Miz Ambrose, called a "descant." Then, come Monday, they'd be looking darts at each other like Sunday never happened.

Addie had had Jesse kill and pluck one of the hens the day before and had cooked it up for Sunday supper. She'd pulled some yams from the root cellar and there was a dab of real butter and fresh boiled greens. For a treat, she'd bartered some hoe cakes with Miz Knox for a small jar of honey which they spread on cornbread. Jesse didn't press her on why she fixed a feast, for that was what it amounted to. Sunday dinners were always the best meal of the week, but he hadn't seen this kind of eating for a very long time. He guessed it was to celebrate the fact that he wasn't in the county pokey anymore.

The evening air had turned chilly and he was restless. He changed out of his Sunday clothes and walked over to the Billingsley place. Hoke and his kin were the most easygoing people on the mountain. If Jesse had any hope of finding some peace and quiet, avoiding the questions and looks, that would be the place to be.

The whole Billingsley clan was gathered on and around the front porch. Hoke played a mean guitar and his brother, Amos, might have been the fiercest banjo picker in all of Floyd County. A couple of cousins, including the Wesley McAdoos, sat nearby with jugs and a tub rigged with a long leather thong fixed to a bow. Wesley could tighten or loosen the bowed arm and change the pitch of the thong he plucked. The boys with the jugs either whomped them like drums or blew across the open end to add a note that defied putting on a scale but mostly sounded like *whoonk*. They were in the middle of a breakdown when Jesse strolled up. Hoke motioned with his head toward a fiddle lying on the porch beside him.

Jesse shook his head. He hadn't done any fiddling since before the war. Someone behind him gave him a little shove in the direction of the fiddle. He shook his head again, but stepped up on the porch, retrieved the mountain Stradivarius and plucked its strings. It was pretty much in tune. Good enough for this crowd, anyway.

Most of mountain music would be played by ear. If there was anybody there who could read music, he sure didn't know who that would be. Even Miz Ambrose, the church organist, had at best only a nodding acquaintance with the dots on the page of sheet music. Jesse picked up the tune and tempo and drew the bow across the strings. Adding the violin to the mix changed the whole composition. The way they played music, always did that. If someone jumped in with a Jew's harp or harmonica, it would shift again. Capturing that on a piece of paper or trying to put it on one of those newfangled Edison disc machines was next to impossible. The basic tune might be the same, but the execution varied from day to day and moment to moment.

They made music for an hour or so and then Hoke broke out a jug of fresh-pressed cider. There'd be no liquor on a Sunday. Well, none anybody would own up to, but there were a few who supplemented their cup of cider from a pocket flask or something poured out of a Mason jar. Wesley McAdoo sat down next to Jesse and nodded a greeting.

"Near thing, yesterday."

"Not as near as it might have been. I still would like to know which one of us signed that witness statement. When did we change our minds about working with the law?"

"It ain't. This is something nobody went in for, and as far as who signed it, you don't want to know, Jesse. You let that dog lie. Knowing can't do anything but pull us apart. We sure don't need any of that now."

"Then I'll let her lie, Wesley, but one day I aim to find out and that person and me will have some words."

"Fair enough." Wesley pulled out a flask and poured out a dollop of clear mountain moonshine into his cider. "You want a snort?"

Jesse held put his cup and Wesley tipped in a taste. "Cider's okay, I reckon, but after a week of busting your back scratching out a living from what amounts to a rock farm, a man needs a little back door medicine, is what I say."

"Amen to that."

"I hear you be working at the sawmill."

"I am."

"They pay good?"

"Not so much good, as fair. It's all you can ask for these days."

"They hiring?"

"Maybe. You could ask."

"It ain't for me. This old hound can't learn no new tricks. I'm thinking on my boys."

"Send them down. I'll see what I can do."

"Maybe. Jesse, one more thing. For your own good, ask yourself what the devil was that Barker boy you saved from Anse's noose doing over on this side of the mountain. He's a Lebrun, Jesse. What the hell…sorry, Lord…what the heck was he doing over here at night?"

"You don't think he—?"

"I ain't suggesting nothing, but like I said, he's a Lebrun."

"The mountain is open to whoever wants to walk on it, Wesley. If you're on the public road, you got as much right as anybody else."

"Hell, I know all that. That's not where I'm going here. Look, you're soft on the Barker girl, I know, but you shouldn't let that get in your way of seeing what's happening."

"What should I be seeing?"

"Holy Ned, for a smart man, you can be dull as mud. Just think about it. Why was he even here? That's all I'm saying."

Wesley stood and shuffled over to his people. Jesse sat and tried to make sense of what he'd said. Wesley wasn't a hothead, but he shared all the prejudices about the Lebruns as nearly everybody else on this side of the mountain. So, what was that all about? Jake was the victim, wasn't he?"

Chapter Twenty-two

Monday morning and the work at the sawmill had to go on as usual but it seemed to bog down every half hour or so. Jesse was aware of some strange looks sent his way from the crew and wasn't sure how to deal with them. There'd been no trial, no evidence of any import to support it, but in the eyes of half the men, Jesse Sutherlin was a killer. Who wants to work with a murderer? Finally R.G. walked out of the office and pulled Jesse aside.

"Jessie, we got a problem. I know you didn't stab that boy and most of the thinking folks hereabout know that, too, but the fact is, we aren't getting any real work done today. I want you to take a couple of days off and let things cool down." Jesse started to protest. "It's for the best. I won't dock your pay. You just get on home and figure getting through the next couple of days and then we'll see."

"Mister Anderson, I ain't got no alternative, if you follow. I work or I'll go crazy."

"Jesse, you have a death sentence hanging over your head. Either you settle this mess and things quiet down, or you get yourself killed, or you make a dash for the county line. I don't see any other…what did you say?…alternatives. You are out of options right now. Me? I have a mill to run and I need the men's minds on their work. Otherwise one of them is going to lose a hand to the saw. They need to be concentrating on it, not on you. Now git. I'll see you come Monday."

Jesse shook his head, started to say something and, realizing R.G. wouldn't budge, walked to the office to punch out. Serena watched him with lowered eyes. Jesse couldn't make out if she was angry at, or sorry for, him. He guessed it didn't matter. Somehow he had managed to get on everyone's bad side. Because he killed Albert, because he didn't, because it couldn't be determined what was what. He waved in the direction of Serena's desk and headed up the mountain.

• • ● • •

Jesse pushed through the branches that screened the copse from the path and saw Big Tom standing by the coil box of his, by now, restored still. Big Tom spun around at the sound of footsteps and reached for his rifle.

"Whoa, it's me, Grandpa. It's Jesse."

"What're you doing here? Why ain't you down in the valley sawing wood? You get yourself fired?"

"Nope. The boss wants me to lay low for a while. Somehow folks latched on to the notion that I was a killer. How do you suppose they came by that idea?"

"Well, in spite of all your bellowing that you ain't, and I don't fault you on that, naturally, you are reckoned to be the man that done in Albert Lebrun and that's a fact."

"And me saying I didn't kill anybody don't make a difference?"

"Well, shoot, Jesse, what kind of a fool would own up to that? A man could get hisself arrested and hung if he did."

"So, you all think that's what I'm doing? Saying I'm innocent just to fool the hangman?"

"Ain't you?"

Jesse sighed and sat on a stump. "It don't make a lick of difference what I say. You all will believe what you will. Maybe Serena's right. I should just pack up and go."

"You ain't planning on leaving. You don't want to do that, Jesse. Everyone will think you're a coward who John Henry called out and you skedaddled."

"So, it's a preference up here in this corner of the world that it's better to be a dead hero than a live coward."

"Well, when you put it that way, yes, by God. And you ain't no coward, everybody knows that."

"Not everybody, Grandpa."

"Well, them people ain't got the sense of a tadpole. You don't pay them no mind. Why you'd come up here, anyway?"

"I come up here to look at the scene of the crime. That's what they call it in them dime novels—the scene of the crime. I'm hoping I missed something the first time."

"What in blazes for?"

"Because, no matter what folks on both sides of the mountain may think, we ain't caught Solomon's killer and I aim to do that if I can. Then I'll get off the mountain and everybody's mind."

"Jesse, I've lived on this mountain all my life. I seen folks come and go, good times and bad. Take my advice, let that dog lie."

"Why is everybody saying that? Leave it lie. I appreciate the thought, but I ain't buying it. Tell me again exactly where Solomon was when you found him."

Big Tom gave Jesse a look that would curdle cream. No one had done a thing like that since he was discharged from the Army. When his gaze had softened sufficiently, Big Tom walked him through what he'd told him five days before—where Solomon had been lying, which way had he been facing when he was shot, the positions of the wrecked still, the lot.

"Thank you, Grandpa. So it appears that whoever shot Solomon must have come up behind him and maybe even followed him here. He'd have come from the path the same as Solomon and..." Jesse walked to the place where he and Abel had found footprints. "Whoever was standing over here most likely had nothing to do with the shooting."

"Someone was standing over there?"

"Yep. Me and Abel found us a double set of footprints that day. They're dried up some, but you can still make them out. If they were the ones doing the shooting, they would have had to come out of the woods and Solomon would have seen them.

It's not likely he'd turn his back on anyone who pushed in here, would he?"

"How the hell would I know that?"

"Just stands to reason. So, okay, what did these two people do?"

Jesse stepped into the woods being careful not to disturb the dried footprints. He brushed aside some leaves.

"Ah, here's something new. I didn't see this because the leaves covered them, but I have more footprints." He stood in a position parallel to the first set, took a step back, and turned. "Whoever these fellers were, they came to the edge here, stopped, and then stepped back." Jesse scrutinized the ground. "I'm guessing they saw something and were frightened by it. They turned and hightailed it back down the mountain. These are not the shooter's footsteps. They belong to a witness. Make that two witnesses. I need to find out whose feet match these prints."

"I swear to goodness, Jesse, why in the world are you still at this?"

"I told you, Grandpa. I want to find out who killed Solomon and if I do, I will also know who killed Albert Lebrun."

"Them two killings ain't related, Jess."

"Not related? Grandpa, you ain't been paying attention. They are hand and glove. Someone shot Solomon in the back. That set a war in place between them and us. Then, Albert is stabbed to death and that don't settle it. Mean and nasty as they can be, the Lebruns know the rules, you could say. If Albert was the one who shot Solomon and was killed in revenge, they'd accept that. Eye for an eye and all that, but if Albert didn't shoot Solomon, then we are in a worse place than before, you see?"

"It's too deep for me. Whyn't you listen to me? Let the thing go. Solomon is dead, a Lebrun is dead. We're done."

"That's where you're wrong. It ain't finished. Don't you understand? John Henry is fixing to stick a knife in my gizzard. If he does, a McAdoo will go off and do in another Lebrun, who will take out two or three McAdoos and it will never end. Unless somebody, I guess that'd be me, figures this out in the next day or so, this mountain will explode and the only people who'll be happy about that are the U.S. of A. Revenue Agents. They will have one less mountain to patrol for bootleg liquor because the only folks left up here will be dead, dying, or widows."

Chapter Twenty-three

Jesse left his grandfather to tend his still and to stew about his grandson's pigheadedness. He cranked up the Model T and drove it to town. He wanted to have a sit-down with Bradford the lawyer. With any luck, he'd catch him in his office and not busy. His luck held and not only was Bradford not in court, but had been about to send for Jesse. He was ushered into an office that, to him, was remarkable primarily for its opulence. For all of his life, Jesse had endured the Spartan existence poverty brings. It wasn't a thing he gave much thought to. It had always been that way. The concept of poor as opposed to something else never entered his thinking. His stint as a soldier and seeing how strange and different the rest of the world was had shocked him almost as much as being shot at by strangers in German uniforms. The notion that some people, many in fact, had all the food and material goods they ever wanted and could get them, and more, whenever they chose, dumbfounded him.

"Jesse, sit and listen. I have two things I think you will want to hear. First, you asked me to look up the Fairchild Leigh deed and documents that placed it in an entailed status. I have done just that. Also, I have the coroner's report for Albert Lebrun's killing. I expect you'll want to read it as well. Both of those documents make for very interesting reading."

"Sir? The Lebrun folk called in the police?" The idea they would do such a thing bordered on the unthinkable. Mountain people settled their own affairs. His run-in with Sheriff Franklin had been shocking as much for the fact of it, than the circumstances which brought it on. Nobody on the mountain willingly cooperated with the police unless they wanted something only the flatlanders' law could give them. Somebody must really want Jesse's neck in a noose.

"Well, of course they did. Now, look here." Bradford shoved a stack of papers across the desk at him. "That top one is especially important."

Jesse picked up the first in the stack and squinted at it. Reading wasn't his oyster but he could usually manage to get the gist of it with some help. He could make out the bold print at the top but the rest seemed a confusion of blurred symbols and lines. He held it closer to his nose. "I can make out it says this here is about the Leigh property." Jesse dropped the paper back on the desk.

"Mister Bradford, I am sorry, but could you read it out for me? I ain't too quick in that department."

"Jesse, do you need spectacles?"

"Me? I never thought about it."

Bradford rooted around in his coat pocket and produced a pair of steel-rimmed glasses. "These are store bought and not too strong. I use them to help me with the small print that some folks have gotten in the habit of inserting in contracts lately. Put them on and look again."

Jesse did as he said and picked up the paper again. This time he could make out the words and read them. The spectacles did the trick.

"Well, looka here. Thank you, Mister Bradford. All this time I thought I was too dense to tackle this reading business. Where can I get me a pair of these?"

"I got them from the Sears and Roebuck catalog. The thing is, you ought to get your eyes tested by the eye doc first. You might need stronger ones or corrective ones."

"No sir, these seem just fine. Sears and Roebuck, you said?"

"Well then, you just keep them. I got me another pair around here somewhere. So what do you see?"

"Well, sir, that's another thing. I can for sure make out the words and could read them off to you, but that don't mean they're making any sense. This document is all in lawyer words, you could say. Maybe you should just tell me what it's about."

Jesse slid the glasses back across the desk.

"No, you keep them. The day will come when they might make the difference between getting rich and going broke. Okay, here's the thing. You knew the land was entailed, right?"

"Yeah. Serena said that was like them kings and dukes who leave all their stuff to the oldest male in the line, or something."

"Close enough. Ordinarily, it is a simple thing, but every entailment is a mite different. This one, for example, stipulated what happened if there is no male heir in the direct line. You understand that?"

"Maybe. Does it mean that cousins and such don't count?"

"Very good. That is exactly what it means."

"So, I heard there wasn't any men in Leigh's line. Does it go to the women next?"

"It could, but there don't seem to be any women either, not counting cousins, of course."

So, then, what happens to the property?"

"Ah, that is where it gets interesting. In this state, property is generally presumed abandoned if it has remained unclaimed by the owner for more than five years after it became payable or distributable."

"What's that mean?"

"It means that if nobody has stepped forward to claim the property five years after the death of the owner, that is if there is no heir apparent, the property reverts to the state for distribution."

"But if there is a woman in the line somewhere, couldn't she ask for the property?"

"She could and she would probably get it. Fact is, nobody has stepped forward. Remember these folks went west and settled there. A tract of land on a played-out mountain in Virginia isn't something for anyone to lust after, now is it?"

"I reckon not, but if they knew the value of the timber on it, they might."

"Jesse, there is something you need to know. Hardly anybody not in the business has the foggiest idea about the value of trees and such. Also, Buffalo Mountain is a far piece to travel to, just to find out there's a few hundred dollars in wood waiting to be harvested on it."

"More'n a few hundred, sir. So, where does that leave us?"

"In a pretty good spot, actually. At my urging, the state has declared a presumption of abandonment on the property. They wouldn't have even noticed before, because the taxes are all up to date. I had to point out to them the owner is long dead and gone. So, as it now stands, anybody who holds an interest, can put in a claim and if it is accepted they can buy it from the state."

"Buy it? What would it cost? Land up there ain't worth a whole lot. Five dollars, maybe ten, an acre is what it goes for nowadays."

"Usually, the state will settle for back taxes due."

"But the taxes have been paid."

"Exactly. That raises an interesting legal question. If the taxes are paid, and in this instance, in perpetuity, what is the state's interest in releasing the land, and if they do so, what happens to the trust that is attached to it?"

"You're asking me? I ain't got the foggiest. What happens?'

"Let me read this. It's in the code." Bradford leafed through a heavy leatherbound book, found the place he was looking for and looked up. "Let me borrow back those glasses for a minute,"

Jesse handed them back. Bradford cleared his throat and read.

A private trust requires a beneficiary that is definitely ascertained at the creation of the trust or definitely ascertainable within the period of the rule against perpetuities. Restatement §112. The members of a definite class of persons can be the beneficiaries of a private trust, but the members of an indefinite class generally cannot be.

Jesse shook his head. "I have no idea what you just read is about. What's that mean exactly?"

"It means that there is sufficient ambiguity here for me to go to a judge and separate the trust from the property. You will jump in and offer to pay the back taxes—"

"But there ain't none."

"There will be the minute I get the separation. There're always taxes due. You pay them and you get the land."

"Well, that's just dandy, but where am I going to get the money for that?"

Bradford sat back in his chair and studied Jesse for a full minute. "Here's what I will do. I personally am not interested in the timber business. I tried it ten years ago and lost a pretty big piece of my shirt. So, here's my offer to you. I will pay the tax on your behalf for a percentage of the profit you make on turning it around. I assume you will sell the timber rights and eventually the land." Jesse frowned at the last. "Or if you keep the land, I expect you'll sell the timber, so I will take ten percent of the profit of either or both. That is an investment in you, you could say."

"Ten percent is pretty steep, sir."

"You have a better plan? Remember I am doing all the legal work here and, to be frank, I could do it without you and take the whole thing for myself and then you'd end up with nothing. So, do we have a deal?"

Without having done a careful inventory, Jesse reckoned there could be as many as ten harvestable trees on each acre, some more, some maybe not as many. That's a hundred trees. Depending on the type, they would go for anywhere between ten and twenty dollars each. The black cherry near the Spring House, for example, was at least six feet around and had no rot. Well, none that he could see. That one alone would sell for a small fortune. So, one hundred trees at an average of twelve dollars plus or minus makes, if he figured it right, twelve hundred dollars. Bradford's cut of that would be one hundred and twenty dollars and the rest would be his.

"Yes, sir, I reckon we do."

Chapter Twenty-four

Bradford tapped a call bell on his desk and moments later, his door opened and the plainest woman Jesse had ever seen entered. She couldn't fairly be described as ugly. She was not. Her plainness had more to do with her mien and dress. In truth, she had that fine bone structure that a dozen years later would define a certain movie star. She wore a dark gray skirt which missed hitting on the floor by no more than a half inch and a marginally lighter gray shirtwaist. Her hair matched her gray outfit and had been pulled back into the tightest bun he'd ever seen. Jesse didn't know much about women, fashion, or hairstyles, but he did wonder if that bun didn't yank her features back so hard as to be painful. The expression on her face suggested it might.

"Miss Primrose, I will need a standard contract establishing a business arrangement between Mister Jesse Sutherlin and myself as regards the distribution of profits from the sale of certain goods and services. Wait, maybe a Memorandum of Understanding would serve better."

"Mister Bradford, if all that chat with Miss Primrose is about what we just made a deal on, it ain't necessary. Where I come from, a man's word is his bond. You shake on a deal, it's done."

"And what if one of the parties doesn't fulfill his end of the bargain?"

"It don't happen. At least not more'n once. If you cheat someone on the mountain, you'd best catch a train to Texas, or

Mexico, or one of them other foreign countries out that way 'cause you can for sure expect to see somebody with a Remington single shot on your doorstep the next day and the undertaker be standing right behind him."

"Miss Primrose, I will not need that writing after all. Thank you. Why don't you take an early lunch?"

The woman graced Jesse with what could pass as a smile… or not…and left.

"What about that trust money which pays the taxes, the trust business? What happens to it?"

"Well, now, here's my idea on that. A piece of land the heirs might have deemed useless won't stir their bones much, but if I separate the money from the land, well, I reckon there will be plenty of interest in the former. If whoever legally owns that land gets the idea there is money that could come their way, why he will be mighty happy to see the property off the books. A smart lawyer will find a way to put all that cash in their pocket, don't you think?"

"And you are the smart lawyer to do that."

"Could be, could be."

"Lordy, you people must take lessons from weasels. You said you saw a coroner's report on Albert Lebrun."

"I did. Not much there. The boy got himself stabbed once in the neck and a couple of times in the chest. The coroner says the neck wound is what killed him, something about being behind the left clavicle…that'd be the collarbone…and the blade cut the ascending aorta, whatever that is. Big blood vessel in the chest up high, they tell me. Doc says he'd have bled to death inside thirty seconds."

"Less time than that. That would have been the first cut. The others are just 'to be sure' stabs."

"To be sure stabs?"

"Yeah. You can't always tell about knife stabbing or any other kind, for that matter. Folks are put together different, so you poke him once and then, when he falls, you stick him once in the heart. In this case seems he got that twice."

"You know that? How?"

"It's what the Army teaches and what every knife-fighter knows if he wants to stay alive."

"If you say so. Does knowing about the wounds help?"

"A little maybe. It would be nice to know the angle the knife made on that neck stab."

Bradford scanned the report. "If I read this correctly, it was straight down or maybe slightly anterior. I think that means toward the front. Mean anything to you?"

"Some. How about the chest wounds?"

Bradford leafed through the pages. "Umm…it says the first was in his right thorax…that's his chest."

"Yes, sir, I know."

"And the other missed the heart as it entered left to right. Neither one of them went in too deep, it says. That's it. Well, I got a date in court in a half hour, Jesse. Good talking to you. I'll let you know about the property settlement as soon as I have something."

The two men stood, shook hands and went their separate way, Bradford to the courthouse and Jesse, home.

Jesse shrugged his coat closer when he stepped out of the Ford. Because of elevation, mountain folks got the change in weather before those in the valley did. It wasn't frost time, but soon would be. A curl of smoke rose from the cabin chimney. A puff of wind blew it away. Jesse caught the scent of burning cherry wood. He walked around back and saw the wood pile had not been tended to. Abel had been off dillydallying, he supposed. Jesse shed his coat, grabbed the axe and began to split wood. His mother peered out the back door, saw him at work, sniffed and disappeared back inside. After he'd stacked a cord of new firewood, Jesse retrieved his coat and went inside.

"There's coffee on the hob," his mother said. "Why ain't you at work?"

"I am something of a celebrated person nowadays, Ma. The boss thought I should lay low for a while."

"So, no fancy new icebox any time soon?"

"I'm still being paid, if that's what you're angling after."

"I ain't, but that's good to know. So, where you been?"

"I had to run down to Floyd to see my lawyer."

"Lawyer? Land sakes. Why?"

"He's helping me look into the Leigh property."

Addie harrumphed. "Seems to me they should have kept calling it Jacksonville. Why'd they change the name of the town to Floyd?"

"To grow and prosper. It's the county motto, ain't it? We're growing and prospering all over the place."

"Stuff and nonsense." Addie studied her son. "You didn't kill that Lebrun boy, did you?"

"No, Ma'am, I did not."

"Well, that's a mercy. I ain't saying that the Lebruns aren't in the need of a good lesson or two, but killing ain't the answer to nobody's problem. It seems to only make for more killing. If you live as long as I have you get weary of it. What is it with men-folks that they think having honor means killing everybody that don't agree with them?"

"Beats me, Ma. All the boys over there in France dying because some stuck-up aristocrat got a bomb dropped in his lap and over who gets to be in charge of what. None of it matches up with common sense, but we go over there to Europe anyway and a whole lot of good men are killed because of it."

"Does that mean you won't be fighting John Henry Lebrun?"

"I hope to goodness I don't have to, but..." Jesse could only shrug his shoulders. Fate, he knew, wasn't too choosy. At the same time he did not have "The Feeling," so maybe not.

"Pshaw, hoping and doing is two different things. You know that. Here, you set a spell and drink your coffee." She handed him a mug with the symbols of the Norfolk and Western Rail Road emblazoned on it. "Your daddy brought that mug back from when he went over to Roanoke to look for work in the locomotive shops. He didn't get the work, but he did bring home that mug."

"I know Ma. It was a favorite of his. I'm afraid I don't have any useful souvenirs from my days traveling for the government."

"You stuffed things from the Army under your bed. What's that if it ain't reminders?"

"Well, there is some wearable clothes. I reckon I could get to wearing them after a bit. Not right now. The leggings aren't worth a hoot, but the boots is sturdy and the rest…well if it weren't so Army, I could wear them. We'll see."

"Waste not, want not, Jesse. If you can't bring yourself to put them on, maybe Abel could. They'll be big on him, but he'll grow into them. Oh, and he didn't want to wear his old coat 'cause it were a mite too small and his wrists stuck out a mile, so I done put one of your Army jackets on him this morning. You weren't using it so I figured he ought to."

"Sure, that's fine, Ma."

Jesse stood and went into the room he and Abel shared as a bedroom. He dragged his backpack and bundle of clothes out from under his bed. The clothes he sorted and put away or hung on pegs. Most of the men returning from overseas were happy to dump their gear on the pier. Some kept their tin hats and, except for the clothes on their backs, little else. Jesse kept it all, even his entrenching tool. The short little shovel had more uses than its name suggested. He lifted out the .32 caliber Colt 1903 semiautomatic pistol he'd been issued when he was promoted. He wished at the time he'd been issued the heavier 1911 forty-five that most of the other officers had, but he wasn't in a position to complain.

He'd inherited his father's old Owlshead revolver. He'd give it to Abel on his birthday in December. The little .32 caliber pistol packed a little more punch and fit snug in his pocket. He'd been lucky with it. The enlisted men had to turn in their rifles and bayonets and most everything else. The officers got to keep their side arms. He put the pistol back in its holster attached to the Sam Browne belt and laid them both in a wooden box which he pushed back under the bed. He took the shovel and his trench knife and went to sit on the porch.

He spent the next two hours sipping coffee and working with a whet stone. John Henry wanted to match blades. Jesse was willing to bet he'd never come across a fight like the one he had in mind.

Chapter Twenty-five

The heavy Mack truck bounced and rattled across the shattered landscape toward the front. Its solid tires rolled over barbed wire as if it was no more substantial than autumn leaves. The truck seemed impermeable to the bullets fired from a dozen German machine guns. Jesse screamed for the truck to stop, to go back. They were all going to be killed. The other passengers, soldiers with their helmets askew, their rifles held upright between their knees, sat stone-faced and silent. He shoved at one and then another, but they didn't say a word. Then, someone tried to stop his shouting. Whoever he or she was shook his shoulder. He shrugged it off. He didn't want to die. Not now, not yet.

"Jesse!"

"Turn around, go back."

"Jesse, wake up. Abel didn't come home last night."

"We're all going to die."

"Sure enough, but not today. Wake up, you hear me?"

Jesse bolted upright. "Ma?"

"You've been having another bad dream, son. The war is over and you're home safe now, thank the Lord. Now, listen to me, Abel ain't here."

"Abel?"

"Come on, boy, wake up. Your brother didn't come home for his supper. He didn't come home at all. I left him a plate, figuring he'd be out carousing with his friends, but every time in the past he done that, he'd get home, eat late, and drop off to bed. His bed ain't been slept in, Jesse. Where's he at?"

Jesse knuckled the sleep out of his eyes. He shook his head and tried to get his bearings. Abel missing? War is over? Right, he knew that. Abel not home. Where was Abel?

"When did you see him last, Ma?"

"About an hour before you came back from wherever it was you went yesterday…Floyd. Abel promised to top off the wood pile. When I heard the chopping, I thought it must be him, but it were you."

"Did he say anything?"

"No. Wait, let me think. Seems like I remember somebody, can't remember who, stopped by and had a quick chat with him. Anse, maybe. No, not him. Well, I don't rightly know, one of them good-for-nothing boys, maybe your Uncle Bob's boy. I can't hardly tell them apart anymore. Well, whoever it was stopped by for a minute and they had some words and Abel up and dashed off like his pants was on fire."

"He didn't say where he was going?"

"Let me think. He maybe went off looking for you. He said it had to do with the fight you got yourself into with that Lebrun boy."

"You're just telling me this now?"

"Well, don't go getting all uppity with me. I figured he found you and that was that. His forgetting to cut firewood wasn't anything new. Staying out late wasn't either. Not coming home, that was."

Jesse rolled out of bed and pulled on his clothes. "I reckon I'll run up to Big Tom's and tell him. Abel's probably sleeping it off somewhere with his knuckle-headed friends. If he's not, we'll put together a search and scour the woods. Don't worry, we'll find him."

Jesse said the words, but somehow, deep down, he didn't believe them. Abel, unlike most of his contemporaries, did not take to drink. He'd have his morning nip and a quick snort now and again, but that was it. He always said it made his head ache, that he got the hangover before he got the drunk. Wherever he was, sleeping it off with his cousins would be the last thing to consider. Still, Ma needed to stay calm. She'd suffered through the war worrying about whether he'd come home from the war alive, broken, or in a box. Now she had Abel to worry her.

Addie had poured him a steaming mug of chicory-laced coffee and laid out some cold pone and bacon.

"You eat that. It ain't much, but if you're going out in the cold, you'll need something between your ribs. There's a jug on the shelf, too."

Jesse wolfed down the corn pone and bacon. He took a swig from the jug, made a face, and topped it off with coffee. "That there wasn't grandpa's whiskey. Where'd you get it, anyway?"

"Well, if you must know, your Pa set up a little still before he went off to Norfolk. He made one batch 'fore he died and that's what's left. I don't believe he had a future in the moonshine business. Son, money was tight and he was willing to try anything, rest his soul."

Jesse gave his mother a grin. "Tell you the truth, I've tasted worse. Not lately, though. Some of that stuff the Frenchies sold us as brandy would curl your toes. It tasted like they cut it with iodine or something."

Jesse opened the door and realized that it had turned bitter cold. Some of the chill would burn off when the sun rose up a bit, but in the early dawn dark, he knew what the coming winter would likely be. He turned on his heel and retrieved his Army greatcoat. Time to stop thinking about France and dead friends and get on with living. That assumed Abel was still among them. He had his doubts about that.

• • ● • •

Big Tom sopped up the last of his beans with a piece of cornbread, no mean feat. Unless you got more egg in it than cornmeal, it'd crumble into mush once it hit the gravy.

"Tell me what you just said and take it slow, this time."

"Abel didn't come home last night. Ma thinks, well she hopes, that he's sleeping it off with some of his cousins, but I don't think that's so. We got to find him, Grandpa."

"You said your Ma thought some boy, one of us, met with him first and then he went off looking for you?"

"Ma thinks so. She didn't know for sure who the boy was, but thought it might be one of them that hangs around with Anse."

Big Tom brushed the crumbs from his beard and stared at a chip in the enameled blue-and-white tin cup on the table in front of him for a minute. Then he twisted in his chair and yelled at a closed door to his right.

"Anse, you get out here this minute."

The door opened and a sleepy Anse McAdoo, clad in long johns and with a blanket draped over his shoulders, stepped out.

"Anse is living with you now, Grandpa?"

"Just for a week or two. With Solomon dead, I need help with the still and, to tell the God's own truth, his Ma could use the rest. Ain't that right, Anse? Your cutting up day and night like to drive your poor old Ma to a full moon loony. So, did any of your block-headed friends stop by the Sutherlins' and talk to Abel yesterday?"

Anse kept his eyes on the floor. Big Tom, they said, was the only person who could shut Anse McAdoo down with a look. If he shouted at him he turned into suet.

"Um…not that I can say. I was working with you most of yesterday, right? I ain't seen much of any of them lately."

"Well you get dressed, grab a bite, and then go round to all of them boys' houses and ask if Abel is staying there. Jesse, you and me will check out a few places soon's it gets light enough to see. If we don't turn up the boy, we'll set up a search and you'd better pray we don't find a Lebrun mixed up in this."

"Grandpa, I know how you all like to think that the folks on the east side of the mountain are to blame for everything from the Crucifixion to the war in France, but this time, how about let's just wait and see?"

"Yeah, yeah, and when it turns out I'm right? What do you plan to do about that?"

"Pinch myself 'cause I'm likely dead."

"There is some days, Jesse, I wonder where your head got to over there in Europe. Maybe you are the one with shell shock and Solomon ended up as the normal one, after all."

"You ain't alone there."

Chapter Twenty-six

By first light, all of the homes where Abel might be staying had been queried. No Abel. Big Tom called in four men and divided the northwest area of the mountain into six sectors. Each man was to select a central point and then walk concentric circles around that point, increasing the distance from it by ten yards or so at each circuit. Only the northern and southernmost would not be double searched as the focal points of all of them were close enough that the outermost ambit of each touched on the next searcher's starting point. Jesse had the point farthest to the south. They agreed that if anyone found anything, they would fire three shots: one, pause, and then two together. If Abel had not turned up in any of the six, they would shift south and begin the process all over again. What they would do if it appeared they needed to search the east side of the mountain was not discussed, although some dark looks were exchanged which suggested that it could be a problem requiring more well-armed searchers. Jesse could only shake his head.

Before taking up his point, he drove to the sawmill. R.G. seemed surprised to see him.

"I thought I told you to take a few days off."

"Yes, sir, you did. I'm not here to work. I came to ask you and Serena if my brother, Abel, happened to come by here yesterday."

Serena had not taken her eyes off Jesse from the moment he entered. "My, my, Jesse Sutherlin, still standing. I thought by now you'd be out on the mountain fighting John Henry or maybe bleeding to death."

"Sorry to disappoint you, but that'll have to wait. Right now, I am looking for my brother who has gone missing. Was he here yesterday?"

"Yes. He stopped by. He seemed to be in a hurry. He said he had to find you, that he had an important message for you or something."

"He didn't say what the message was about?"

"Not to me."

"Nor me," R.G. added.

"Damnation, what has that lunkhead got himself into now?"

Jesse left the mill and drove back up the mountain, parked, and began his search. His point, the pivot for his circular swing, was the Spring House. Jesse wondered at that. It seemed like this chunk of mountain had way too much to do with him lately. Was he being given a sign? He didn't truly believe in Divine Intervention, well, not in the puny matters of ordinary folks, anyway, but the Spring House just seemed to figure in too much in the flow of things over the last week to be a complete coincidence. He paced off ten yards to the east, turned left, and began his first counter-clockwise orbit around the Spring House. When he'd completed it, he paced off another ten yards farther east and walked the woods again.

On his fifth circuit, he could see Ogden Knox in the distance. Knox had started earlier, while Jesse was at the mill, and was further along in his search. Jesse kept moving, his eyes darting first right then left, walking and probing the underbrush. The turn brought him to the creek the locals called Catfish because if you were desperate for something to eat, you could almost always catch you one of them with not much more than a worm for bait. He paused and then decided it might be useful to search its banks. It ran southeast before it turned west. All of the creeks, streams, and rivers in Floyd County flowed west, their waters ultimately joining the Mississippi River. He'd need to take care moving eastward, if only temporarily, or he might find himself in Lebrun territory. Well, what of it? Nobody was about to do anything to him anytime soon. At least not until he and John Henry had done their best to gut one another. Until that happened, there would be a ceasefire on the mountain of sorts. Crazy way to make peace.

He'd gone something less than a hundred yards, had found nothing, and turned to retrace his steps when he heard a rustling in the underbrush. His hand dropped to grip the little Colt he'd the foresight to put in his pocket. Jake Barker stepped out in the open.

"Holy cow, Jake, you like to get yourself shot dead, sneaking around like that."

"Jesse. I ain't aware of any sneaking. Hey, I've been looking for you all over the place. You weren't to home. Your Ma wasn't exactly polite, by the way. Serena said you went to the mill and left, but didn't say where to. I'd about given up and was on my way home when I heard folks crashing around in the woods and came to see if it was you, and here you are. What are you doing this far away from your house?"

"My brother, Abel, is missing. A bunch of us are searching for him. You didn't happen to run across him in your travels, did you?"

"Nope, sorry."

"Well, I wandered down this creek thinking I might find a footprint or something. I was just heading back. Why were you searching for me?"

"I came to warn you. When you meet with John Henry later today, you won't be alone. Every able-bodied Lebrun and some that ain't, but hanker after them, will be lurking in the woods. Watching John Henry, you could say, making sure you don't do anything dirty. I told them you'd be last person in the county to cheat, but they weren't the convinced. The betting is that John Henry will beat you fair and square, but if that ain't the case, they plan to make sure you're dead anyway. Don't fight him, Jesse. You can't win even if you do."

"Lord have mercy. There's no end to this foolishness, is there? Well, here's a little something to take back to them. Unless I miss my guess, the other half of the woods will be chock full of McAdoos, too. That means win or lose, all kinds of hell is coming to the mountain unless somebody or something happens along to stop it."

Jake's shoulders slumped. "You should have let those boys string me up when you had the chance. That way I don't have to be a part of all this stupid."

"You don't mean that."

"No, probably not, but there's days when I wonder."

"Exactly. So, here's the rest of what I want you to take back to your side of the mountain. There won't be a fight today or tomorrow. It will have to wait 'til Saturday. I need to settle what happened to Abel first. It's about family and I reckon you all can understand that. Also, I won't be at the Spring House or in the woods. You tell John Henry that if he wants to fight me, he should go clear up to the summit. There ain't no trees up there that amount to much, no hiding places for friends and relations, if you follow me. There's a meadow-like stretch of land that runs down the south side for maybe twenty yards or so and it flattens out near a little stream. This time of year it won't have much water in it. It'll be mostly mud. Anyway, that's where I will meet him. If he still wants a fight, it'll have to be there and nowhere else. Then tell the Lebruns and their kin that they are welcome to tag along, but no hunkering down in the bushes. Stand out in the open like grown men. I will tell the McAdoos to do the same. Everything and everyone out in the open. No tomfoolery. You got all that?"

"I got it. Jesse, why don't you just take Serena's advice and skedaddle?"

"Because, Jake, it would solve my problem, but nobody else's. Sooner or later, this crazy way we live has got to stop. I leave, what's to stop the next gang of idiots from stringing you up for no other reason than you being from the wrong side of the mountain?"

"Nothing, I guess. Okay, Saturday, meadow on the south side just down from the top of the mountain."

"Where it levels out. Saturday, noon."

"Noon, Saturday, right. Serena won't be happy."

"Well, that's no surprise. Not much I do pleases her, nowadays."

"You got the wrong end of the stick there, Jesse." Jake turned and walked away into the trees.

Wrong end of the stick?

Chapter Twenty-seven

Jesse retraced his steps to back to the point where he'd moved off his course. He'd taken a step toward the north when he heard the gunshots—one, pause, and two more in quick succession. Someone had found something. Abel? He rushed in the direction of the sound. He glimpsed Hoke Billingsley way off to his right.

"Over here."

Jesse and four others converged on a bluff which hung over a creek. Abel lay on his back at the bottom, his head on the bank. Water washed over the rest of him. Jesse slid down the bank. Abel was ice cold. Was he dead or was lying in the water all night the reason? Jesse prayed it was the water. He sure seemed deathly pale.

"Is he alive?" Big Tom yelled.

Jesse felt for a pulse. He couldn't be sure. He leaned over Abel and tried to listen for a breath. It was possible he heard a sigh. He felt Abel's neck the way he'd seen medical orderlies in France do. There was a faint throbbing.

"I think so."

Jesse rolled Abel very gently to one side. He saw the knife wound in his left shoulder and the bloody gash on the back of his head.

"He's been stabbed and he's got a helluva wound on his head. He must have hit it on a rock when he fell down the bluff."

"Jesse, there ain't no rocks on that fall except the river rocks he's lying on and his head didn't make it to the water."

It was true. The slope was clay mixed in with a few bits of flint none of which were large enough to have caused the gash on the back of Abel's head. Jesse could see the path Abel's body took on its trip down. It started about halfway up from the bottom. He guessed that meant Abel had been shoved after he'd been stabbed and hit with a rock or stick.

"Look around and see if you see a rock of length of tree branch with maybe some blood on it up there."

"You think someone hit him? Why stab and hit? If he had, wouldn't he have chucked the rock in the creek?"

"Maybe. Come on down here and help me bring him up."

Hoke held up a rock. "I reckon this is the one."

They managed to rig a rough stretcher with saplings cut into six-foot lengths and coats buttoned and stretched across them. Getting Abel up the incline turned out to be more of a struggle than they had thought.

"Your brother needs to trim a few pounds, Jesse."

"We'll have a chat about that, Hoke, but you understand, it might be awhile 'fore I do."

They managed to work the stretcher up the slope and between the six of them taking turns, carry Abel home.

Granny Parkins was sent for and she arrived carrying the poke which contained the items she called her "Fixins." No one really knew what lurked in its depths but whatever it or they were, the poultices and tisanes concocted from them were considered miraculous. Doctor Barney, the local quack would have none of it, of course. But if you needed a bone set, a fever reduced, suffered the worst effects of most diseases, or needed a baby delivered, Granny Parkins got the call. If she weren't available, well, then you called Doc Barney and heaven help you.

"This boy has a lump on his head that has caused him to lose his senses. 'Course you know that already. I can patch him up. I can stitch up the cut in his back, which ain't that bad, but whether he ever comes back from where he's at, only time will tell. Now you all get out of here and let me work. Addie Sutherlin, you boil up some water and put these cloth bandages in it.

When they been cooked proper, you wring them out and bring them to me. Be careful you don't scald your hands. I don't need two hurt folks to work on, you hear me?"

Jesse and Big Tom sat on the porch. The other four said they'd pray for Abel and drifted off. Jesse thanked them for their help.

"Family is family," Hoke said.

"Now you tell me something, Jesse, who did this?"

"I know what you want to believe, Grandpa. You could be right, but there is a niggling around in the back of my mind and it tells me something just ain't right about this whole damned business."

"By Gadfrey, something's not right and you know what it is."

"No, that's the point. I do not know who, or what it is. Look at what we do know, Grandpa. Put your lifelong hatred for Lebruns and their kin to one side for a minute and listen. First, Solomon is shot in the back while working on your still. The Lebrun people may know you have one, but what are the chances they know where it's at?"

"Any fool can find out if they want to."

"Maybe they can and maybe not. You are pretty tight about where you put it. Ain't but a half dozen people know. That's not the point, anyway. The first thing you gotta ask is why? I said it before and I say it again. They may be as rotten bad as Judas hisself, but they are not stupid. If they wanted to kill one of us, they'd fix up a reason and then do it. They are not blockheaded enough to sneak over from the other side, kill Solomon, and rabbit back home. Also, Albert swore it wasn't any of them and he had no reason to lie. For that matter, to even to come and talk to me. It just don't make any sense."

"Jesse, you have been away. You has forgot what it's like here."

"No, not so. Listen to me. Why was Albert Lebrun killed? Nobody over here claims they did it. That's the second thing. As much as you and the others might want to believe it, I didn't kill him. So who did and why? It's the *why* in all of this that I don't get. And now Abel is knocked into next week, stabbed, but not deep, and tossed over the bluff. A little farther out or facedown and he's dead."

"Jesse, you don't know—"

Addie stepped out on the porch. "You two need to shut your clap traps for a minute and tell me what this means. We found it in Abel's pocket."

She handed Jesse a slip of paper which had only managed to survive ten hours of creek water because Abel had put in his top pocket of his overalls.

"What's it say?"

"Give me a second, Grandpa." Jesse squinted at the paper. He rummaged around in his shirt and found the glasses Nicholas Bradford had given him. He perched them on his nose and read. "It says, 'Jesse,' That's me. Hmm. 'If you want to know who really killed Albert Lebrun. Meet me on the path to the Walker place at seven tonight.' The words are sorta scrambled and, I ain't no expert, but not much on their spelling either, but that's the drift."

"When did you start wearing specs?" Addie asked.

"Pretty recent, actually. Lawyer Bradford gave them to me. All them years of being yelled at by schoolteachers and told I was a lunkhead and turns out all I needed was to see better."

Big Tom stamped his foot. "Never mind all that, what about the note?"

"You didn't ever get that note did you?"

"No, Ma, I didn't. It looks like Abel searched and couldn't find me and figured it was so important, he'd go to the meeting himself. It was me who was supposed to be at the bottom of that little cliff. He musta stood there waiting wearing my coat and some skunk came up behind him. Stuck him in the back. That old Army coat don't look like much, but it is pretty thick wool. You'd need a sharp knife and some pushing to do any real damage. It looks like whoever had the knife found out it wasn't working and bounced a rock off his head. Be nice to know if he got a lick in hisself 'fore he tumbled over. Anyhow, that's how come we found him out there."

"You're saying he's in that bed in a bad way because you was high-stepping off to Floyd?"

"Sorry, but it appears so."

"Sweet Jesus."

"Sorry, Ma, you know Abel. He's always wanted to be a help."

"He looks up to you, Jesse. If you told him to eat a live copper head snake, he'd do it."

"I would never ask him to do anything that would put him in harm's way. You all know that."

Addie's gaze had shifted to the woods across the dirt road that passed by her house. She turned and faced the two men in her life she loved most. In the half light her face looked like it had been carved from quartz. "It ain't right, you hear me? All this killing and fussing over who is what. This is not the way the good Lord laid it out for his children. Buffalo Mountain ain't no Eden, but it ain't supposed to be hell, either. Why did you men let that happen? What is it with you?"

"Ma, I'm trying."

"And not succeeding, and Pa, you ain't doing much to help."

"What are you on about, girl?"

"I ain't no girl anymore, am I? Pa, Jesse, I can't tell you two what to do. Pa, 'cause it's not my place, and Jesse, because you're a grown-up man now, but I am begging the both of you. You got to put and end to this. You two are the only ones on this here mountain with enough sense and grit to get it done. So, you all stop your fussing at each other and go do it."

Chapter Twenty-eight

Addie huffed back into the house. The front door slammed behind her. The two men stared at each other for a minute. Finally, Big Tom spoke.

"So, what do you make of that there screeching?"

"Grandpa, that weren't screeching, that was the sweet voice of reason."

"What?"

"She's right. If there is ever going to be a change come to this damned mountain, you're going to have to be a part of making it happen."

"Me? I ain't going to change a gol'durned thing and you watch your language. I know you been over the ocean and rubbing elbows with soldiers of all sorts, but that don't give you no leave to use the Lord's name in vain."

"Sorry. You're right. At the same time, it's because I have rubbed elbows with other people not from the mountain that I have a view of what's going on here that is different, and I am telling you straight out, this way of living ain't going to last. It can't. The world has been stood on its ear ever since President Wilson sent us over there to fight the Germans. Don't you understand? The world has got smaller and us feuding with the Lebruns is like from another century."

"What in tarnation do you mean, smaller? It ain't shrunk one inch that I can see."

"Not that way. I mean...look, when I was in school, there was this map up on the wall. You could see all the countries in the whole world. There was like fifty-some of them. If I remember rightly, Germany was green, England was sort of red, France was another color. And that's all we knowed about any of them. They were far away. They talked funny and ate frogs legs and such. They were just damned foreigners and didn't mean nothing to us. That is not true anymore. England is a country which, from the peek I got of it from the troop ship, looked pretty much like the U.S. of A. And you know what? So did France. The people, too. If you met them on the street of Roanoke and you didn't hear them talk them languages they do, you couldn't tell them from us. They could as easy be McAdoos, or Lebruns, or Knoxes, or Barkers. When the influenza hit, it got near everybody. Them over there and us over here. We were lucky. Us being on this here mountain sort of protected us, you know. Did you hear that in New York City alone there was in a six-week stretch something like thirty thousand folks died? Maybe a whole lot of millions all over the world in the time 'til it run its course. They didn't just kill off the Germans or the folks in New England. Everybody, my Pa included, got struck down. It was a worldwide thing, see? That's what I mean."

"Jesse—"

"No, let me finish. I know this mountain means the world to you, but it ain't the world and the piddly little set-to's we have up here don't amount to a pile of horse manure in the big scheme of things. What's a half dozen of us dead and cold against thirty thousand? When you all talk about the Lebruns, you make the same damned mistake as all the dopes, and politicians, newspaper writers, and big shots up in New York City. You see differences instead of likes."

"Wait just a dang minute."

"No, I'm done waiting. I seen what hatred that is ponied up by people who plan on profiting from other people's misery does. There's too many men my age pushing up daisies over there in France because the people who could have sat down and settled the mess thought their puffed up pride was more important than the lives of a couple million men. No, sir, I will not wait. If you haven't got the sense God give you to see the light, then I'll do this thing by myself."

"Just you wait a minute. Who do you think you're talking to? What gives you the Almighty right to call down this life as dead? It ain't dead, you hear me? We been on this mountain—"

"Since Hector was a pup. Yeah, I know. And ain't nobody going to push you off. I know that, too. At the same time, except nowadays there is telephones, pictures that move and they say they'll talk someday. There's talk of paved roads, and hospitals, folks on the east talking on the radio and them on the west listening, everybody chugging around in automobiles and… Don't you see? You can have this life, but there's more. More, Grandpa. You don't have to lose anything. What you have can just get bigger. What's wrong with that?"

"Bigger?"

"Well, you know what I mean."

"And what does all this 'bigger' cost? You know there ain't no such thing as a free lunch. What's the cost?"

"You have to give to get, right? 'Give, and it shall be given unto you; good measure, pressed down, and shaken together, and running over, shall men give into your bosom.' That'd be Luke talking."

"I heard that somewhere. What do I give?"

"You'd have heard it in church one of the times you actually went, which, as everybody knows, ain't often. So, you give up the notion that the east side of the mountain and the west side are somehow, some way always going to be enemies. That if a person happens to be named Lebrun it don't automatically mean he's fixing to do you harm. It means you take a breath afore you pop off about what you know when you don't know nothing. That's for starters."

"You can't talk to me like that."

"I can and I am. Listen to me, Grandpa, I been where they done killing wholesale, where boys were dropping like mayflies.

You ever see a man hanging on barbed wire calling for his momma and you know he's gut shot and won't ever see morning? It ain't pretty. Then I get back, safe and sound from that madness and what do I find? My own grandpa is playing like he's the damn King of England and Garland Lebrun is the Kaiser. The killing over here is just the same as over there. I don't know why the rest of them folks and you are fixing to fight and none of you have a notion of why, but you are. It's just like the Mister Wilson's war."

Big Tom sat quietly for a moment. He pulled a crusted old pipe from his bib overall pocket and stuffed a wad of Bull Durham in the bowl.

"You got a match?"

Jesse flicked the phosphorous head of a strike anywhere and held it out for the old man. Big Tom tilted his head and drew in the flame. The tobacco lit and he puffed for a few minutes. Jesse waited and then sat back.

"By golly, Jesse Sutherlin, that's more words out of your mouth than you've spoke in a month."

"Yeah, well...Ma said it was up to you and me to make that go away...you and me. I'm willing. Are you?"

"What the hell can I do?"

"Make people talk to me. Somebody stabbed Albert Lebrun. I told you it wasn't me. Who done it? Ask around and find out who was where when Solomon was killed, when Albert was stabbed. People know things. They'll talk to you."

"And you?"

"I'll find a way back to the other side and ask the same things. It won't be easy. Albert was ready to help me and then he's killed. I got to find me another person who'll help."

"Your Ma said you was sparking that Barker girl. Maybe she'll talk, ask your questions for you."

"We ain't sparking. If we was, we ain't now and sure, maybe someday folks will take women seriously. Maybe now they will, since they got the vote and all, but not on this mountain and not today. She's got a brother, though. I can talk to him. He's already sent me a warning. So, that's something."

"That's the boy you rescued from Anse and broke his wrist doing it? What kind of warning?"

"That's him and the warning can wait."

"Hmmm…Anse is a proper jackass, no doubt about that. You shouldn't have broke his wrist, though."

"Grandpa, he was fixing to stick me with a knife. My other choice was to cut his damn throat."

"Language Jesse, language. What else?"

"Am I going to do? Come Saturday noon, if I have no good answers, I will fight John Henry Lebrun, that's what."

Big Tom tapped out his pipe and stood. "You get on inside and see to your brother. I'll walk around tomorrow and ask a question or two. You be careful, son. We don't want to lose you now you come back. Your Ma near to died every time she seen anything that looked like a telegram truck. Good night."

Chapter Twenty-nine

Jesse reentered the cabin. He avoided his mother's eyes. Abel lay half dead because he, Jesse, had been off the mountain at Floyd trying to get rich instead of being where he should have been.

"It ain't your fault, Jesse."

"But it is. I wasn't here for him and he went off half-cocked like he does. He got himself in this pickle 'cause of me and that's the bare-faced truth."

"The trouble with young'uns these days, Sister Addie," Granny Parkins said, "is they don't have no perspective."

"What in the name of Goodbye Bill does that mean?"

"It means, if you live long enough, you will soon or late learn something. What you, young man, needs to learn is that there is some things you can't see coming and even if you do, you can't do nothing to stop'em. Your brother was going to get hisself into a scrape over you 'fore the year was out. You could bet money on it. It were his nature, Jesse Sutherlin, and that's what I mean. It just happened that yesterday was the day he done it. So, you just pull yourself together and do what you need to do to make sure he didn't get his head busted for nothing."

"That there is your *perspective* on the matter?"

"It is. Now, Sister Addie, you keep your Abel quiet and comfortable. He got himself a fierce whack on his head, but he ain't going to die. He'll sleep that way for a while...a week maybe two, maybe not so long, and then he will come around and want a stack of flapjacks a foot high."

"You're sure about that?"

"As sure as I can be. And you, Jesse Sutherlin, you git out the door and do what you have to do."

"Yessum."

Addie stepped toward him and looked him square in the eye. "It ain't your fault."

"You said so."

"It is so." She put her hand on his shoulder. "I don't want to lose you, Jesse. I done lost your Pa, come close with Abel. So..." She handed him his pistol. "You put this away when you come in. I want you to keep it with you from now on, you hear?"

"I will, but my insides is telling me I won't need it."

"Well you can listen to them all you want, but your Ma is telling you to be on the safe side and carry that shooting pistol."

Jesse left. The chill air nearly knocked him back indoors. The temperature seemed like it had dropped ten degrees in the last hour.

"It's surely the start of a mountain winter." Granny Parkins had followed him out. "You been away for a while. You forgot."

"Everybody keeps saying that. Granny, I been back on the mountain near a year. I didn't leave any memories back in France. I ain't forgot a thing. Why does everyone think I have?"

"I reckon it's 'cause you have changed. I will tell you one thing you for sure have forgot."

"And what is that?"

"You done forgot who you used to be. You come back a changed man. War will do that to you. You go off a boy and come home a man. You used to be full of piss and vinegar, you and you brother, both. There weren't a scrape bit of tomfoolery that didn't include you. You was a wild one, you was. Now, you are somebody new. I'll say a good new, but different. See how that works? Because you don't act like you done in the past, folks naturally think you done forgot everything, but you didn't. No sir, it's all stuck up in your head there somewhere. Only now, you look at it different. You have got yourself some perspective and it's making folks nervous, that's all."

"Abel said something like that the day Solomon get himself killed."

"Sister Sutherlin didn't raise up no dunces."

"Right. So, that's it? Just what do I do with this perspective business?"

"Put it to use. Go find out who done all these bad things lately. Everybody who's here only has one view. You are fitted up better than that."

"I'm sorry, Granny, but I ain't getting this."

"Jesse Sutherlin, what you need to find out is the why. Ain't that what's been bothering you here lately? All this killing and banging people in the head don't make no sense. Them that has never left these parts naturally jump to the same old conclusions they always do and they get into the same old trouble they always did. These men never talk out a trouble. Just yank out your pistol and convince the other feller of your rightness by putting a hole in him. You? Well, you don't see it that way no more because you got—"

"Perspective. That's it?"

"Yep. " She pulled the purse strings tight on her poke. "Why, Jesse Sutherlin, ask yourself why."

• • ● • •

An hour later, Jesse found his way to the Barker cabin. He knew Serena would still be at work, but he hoped Jake might be home. He guessed that the Lebruns and all those loyal to them would be okay with him roaming into their territory. He wouldn't be stabbed, knifed, or bludgeoned today. Funny thing, it had not always been this way, no matter what his kin said. He remembered being ten or eleven and all the kids caroused around together, Lebrun and McAdoo alike. The parents didn't exactly approve, but didn't stop them. When you're young, you don't know how to hate. You learn that later from grownups. He pulled up a memory of a gangly legged Serena with her skirt tucked up and running like the wind across old man Billingsley's pasture. She could beat any boy her size and most of the bigger kids as well. The Billingsleys had to sell the pasture off when the old man came down with consumption and couldn't work anymore. Jake would have been just a tadpole back then.

"Hello, Jesse. Are you lost?"

"Jake. You keep sneaking up on me. It'll get you killed someday, sure. Okay, I come over to see if you and me could have a talk. Are you up for that?"

"Sure, but maybe not here out in the open. How about you come on inside and we'll have a pull or two on a jug and you can tell me what you want."

"I can do that."

They spent the next several hours speculating on what could have prompted someone to do all the things that happened. Jake kept throwing the jug on his shoulder and pulling a swig. After a while his words started to slur and Jesse never got an answer to how it came to be that Jake ended up on the horse with a rope around his neck that night. It was a question that had bothered him since Wesley McAdoo raised it to him on Sunday.

About the time Serena came home from the sawmill, Jake had dropped off. Serena, on the other hand, was her usual sharp-as-a-tack self. Jesse told her about Granny Parkins and what she'd said. Serena listened and nodded her head.

"It's true, Jesse. I reckon that's what has got everyone so off center when it comes to you. Some of the boys over here, like poor dead Albert, had the same problem. They were changed by the war and folks couldn't understand."

"No, not just the war. That is a big part of it, for sure. And it's living in different places where they got different ideas and such. I had to get off this mountain to make a friend with a name like Chiparelli, or Hagström, with two little dots over the O, or a feller who could have been a Chinaman, for all I knew. They all talked different and, by damn, they said it was me that talked funny. You see what I mean? Then you tack on the war. Anybody who says they went to war and didn't come out different is a liar, or he never went."

• • ● • •

It had turned dark by the time Jesse found his way back home. His mother waved him over to the table where she'd laid out a plate for him. Somewhere she'd got hold of a pork chop and added a boiled yam and poke greens. It had been a while since he'd eaten this good. He did not ask where the meat came from. His Ma had her ways. It was something that came with being a mountain woman. They all seemed to have the gift to tap into a little magic every once in a while. No man with any sense ever questioned it.

After he'd eaten, he took his coffee mug, the Norfolk and Western one, and wandered into the bedroom. Abel hadn't moved, as far as he could make out.

"How is he?"

"Addie looked up from her perch on the side of the bed.

"I think I might have seen his eyes flutter a bit. Maybe." A tear ran down her cheek.

"He's going to be alright, ain't he, Jesse? I can't stand the thought of losing another one."

"I ain't dead. What other one?"

"Before you was born, we had us a baby. He died sudden like in his crib. We called him Billy, but he never lived long enough to answer to it."

"I didn't know. You never said."

"You're right, Jesse, I never said because it still hurts my heart, just thinking on it and it didn't help you none to know. And now, it's Abel."

"Ma. Sutherlins is tough people, right? He's going to be just dandy, you'll see. Hey, who's everybody says has got the hardest heads on the mountain? Sutherlins, that's who. He'll be up and making a nuisance of himself any minute now."

"You go on now."

"It's true, Ma, and—"

"You don't need to perk me up, Jesse. I wasn't born yesterday. He's in the Lord's hands now. If it's his time to go to his maker, well, he'll go. If it ain't, he'll come around in his own good time. You, on 'tother hand, need to get to work on who done this. I am tired of saying it. You got to put a stop to this."

"Yessum, I am working on it, for sure."

Chapter Thirty

The next morning Jesse woke before sunup. He lit a lantern and found his way out into the chill predawn air to the privy. When he came back in, he found his mother sitting in her rocker by the stove, still as a stone. He guessed she'd not slept all night.

"Abel seems the same, Ma. He's sleeping peaceable enough." Addie lifted her hand an inch or two in reply, but remained silent.

"Can I fix you something? I'll brew us up a pot."

Jesse put the pot on to boil and measured out a large spoonful of already ground coffee. When the water began to boil he dropped in the coffee and pulled the pot to one side. Back when times were better he'd have added an egg, but not now, not yet. If everything settled down and the job at the mill didn't go away, then he'd see about buying some chickens, It'd be nice to have some laying hens again, but not just now. He put a frypan on the stovetop. He stirred up the coals, which had been banked for the night and added several sticks of wood. They flared and the stove seemed to come to life. Next he sliced a rasher or two from the side of bacon hanging in the corner and put in to fry. He found a pan of cake pone and cut chunks off. He smeared bacon grease on them and placed them on a cracked plate for himself and his mother.

"Thankee, Jesse. You're a good son."

Jesse nodded. They ate in silence. Sunlight crept in under the door sill which reminded him that he needed to tack a slat across the bottom to keep the cold out. Winter was coming.

"Ma, supposing we are going about this all backwards."

"How so?"

"I don't know, exactly, but so far what I've been doing ain't come to anything. Here's what I got to thinking about late last night. Do you remember all the fuss back years ago about the feuding over in West Virginia and Kentucky, them Hatfields and McCoys?"

"I do, maybe not so much, though."

"Well, I met this man on the boat going to France. One day we both of us had got us a leave and somehow I ended up sitting with him in the little eating place they called a café, which is how they say coffee, too, which is a mystery to me. I guess it must be because that's one of the things they sell. Mostly wine as near as I can figure, though. Anyway, when he found out I was from the hills, he got real chatty. He said his Pa worked in the newspaper business. He said all that fussing that was wrote about the feuding over there was mostly made up by folks that had never even set foot out there in the hills in West Virginia and Kentucky. They made most of it up based on a telegram some Jasper sent them and not that many. He said they padded the story up a lot to sell papers, but the whole thing was really all about putting in a railroad along that river and that meant grabbing land. He said he guessed the Peabody Coal Company was mostly responsible for the ruckus. They saw money under the ground out there and aimed to take it."

"Well, I can't say much about that. Seems like one damyankee or another is always poking their fingers in the doings of us folk when there's money to be had. Same as when we had Reconstruction. I guess that there program has just never ended. What's your point?"

"I ain't sure I have one, only...Suppose all this trouble isn't what it seems or what somebody wants it to seem. Like the Hatfields and McCoys. If you got yourself a feud going on, don't it stand to reason that the best way to cover up a murder would be to stir up the feud some, get everybody helloing around about who they hate and what they're going to do to settle the score?"

"I ain't following you."

"What I am wondering about is, suppose all this, the shooting of Solomon, killing Albert Lebrun, and Abel in a bad way, has nothing at all to do with us or the Lebruns. I wonder if we are chasing our tail like a flea-bit dog."

• • ● • •

Jesse knew he needed to stay on the mountain and keep trying to untangle the mess he'd made of things, but at the same time he thought that he might do better if he put some distance between it and himself for an hour or two. He needed to take a long look, gain perspective.

Once he'd settled Abel and tidied up, he dressed and drove his Ford T model to Floyd. Miss Primrose said Lawyer Bradford was not available and that in future, Jesse should call or write ahead of time and schedule an appointment. Jesse said that might pose a problem because telephones were in short supply up on the mountain and writing a letter assumed skills that might not be been available just now. He'd turned on his heel and had reached the door when Bradford came out of his office.

"Is that you, Jesse Sutherlin? Come on in. I might have some news for you. Miss Primrose, this here is Jesse Sutherlin. He is a client and a business partner. He doesn't need an appointment. You ring him in when he comes by when I'm here."

Miss Primrose sniffed and focused her attention on a stack of what Jesse supposed were, probably lawsuits, or contracts, or the other things that occupied a lawyer's time. He took a seat and waited as Bradford lifted one stack of papers and then another, from the right side of his desk to the left.

"It's in here somewhere," he said and moved another pile this time left to right. "Ah, here it is. This is a judgment I managed to squeeze from Judge Watkins to declare the land abandoned and the trust separated from the title. So, we are now officially in business."

"That didn't take too long. I didn't think you could get her done so quick."

"Well, normally, I couldn't, but the judge has an Achilles' heel, you could say."

"Sorry, what?"

"It refers to a vulnerable spot. It comes from *The Iliad*, you remember?"

Jesse did not remember. He allowed as how that was where "it's Greek to me" must have come from and said so. Bradford slapped his knee.

"By Godfrey, you're the real goods, Jesse. I don't know half a dozen men who are willing to confess they don't know something. You stay that way. It'll keep you out of trouble in the long run. Good Lord, an honest man."

"Nope. A Buffalo Mountain man. With a few notable exceptions, we're mostly all like that."

"Which explains why you are a doomed race, Jesse."

"Doomed? How are we doomed?"

"The world isn't ready for honesty just now. Since they hung Jesus on a tree, honesty is a hard commodity to come by."

"I don't understand, why not?"

"Because, Jesse Sutherlin, mountain man, most folks are afraid if they really practice what they preach, they'd end up by being nailed up there with Him. Nobody is looking for that kind of hurt anymore."

"That doesn't make sense, if you don't mind my saying so."

"No, you are correct, it does not, but there it is. So, the good judge has a weakness, his Achilles' heel, like I said, is for real sour mash bourbon whiskey and I happen to have access to a stash of pre-Prohibition hooch, the real Magee, with a label and everything. A bottle of it and my request was expedited, you could say."

"He took a bribe?"

"Shhhh...Never use that word in a lawyer's presence. It could have serious and decidedly adverse effects on the health of the hearer. Let's just say it was merely a gift to thank the judge for the kind thoughts he wrote to me on his last Christmas card."

"He sent you Christmas card?"

"He might have. Who's to say he didn't? Now, as soon as the thing clears, I will scoot down to the courthouse and get us a piece of land which has, as you report, some very fine marketable trees on it."

Chapter Thirty-one

By mid-afternoon the sun had managed to burn off any fog that might have lingered in the dells and the wind subsided to a gentle breeze. If he didn't know better, Jesse would have sworn it was June or late May, not early autumn. He parked the Ford next to his cabin, checked in on Abel—no change there—and set off to find Sam Knox. He still wanted to know what Jake Barker had been up to on the west side of the mountain that ended up with him being ambushed by Anse McAdoo and his friends. He knew Anse would never tell him, but Sam might. Sam wasn't the smartest hound in the pack and because of that Jesse guessed he would be a mite more open to answering a few questions than any of the others. He had better be.

He knocked on the Knoxes' door. Weezy Knox answered. She gave Jesse a hard look. He guessed Sam had given his Ma an edited version of what had happened that night.

"Afternoon, Miz Knox, I was wondering if you could tell me where I might find Sam."

"He ain't here and even if he was, I surely wouldn't tell you, Jesse Sutherlin."

"No, Ma'am. Why is that?"

"He said you was the one who cuffed him about 'tother night."

"That is true. I did do that. Did he tell you that I did it because he happened to be holding the reins of a horse that had a man sitting on it whose hands were tied up and who had a noose around his neck ready to be hanged? Him and his friends were fixing to lynch a feller from over on the other side of the mountain. Did he happen to mention that?"

"I don't believe you."

"No, I expect you don't. If I was his Ma, I wouldn't want to think that it would be possible for my boy, either. Trouble is, that's what he done. I don't know if he would have gone through with it, of course. I hope not, but at the time, I couldn't take a chance. When he wouldn't let go of the bridle when I asked him to, I had to give him a swat. I don't believe it hurt any more that the Saturday licking his Pa generally deals out, do you?"

Louise Knox stared at Jesse for a spell, turned, and before she shut the door said, "He's down in the meadow plowing. That's where he's supposed to be, anyway. If he ain't there, your guess is as good as mine. His Pa needs to put a leash on that boy 'fore he turns out bad as his cousin Anse."

Jesse did not find Sam in the meadow, although the Knoxes' mule was there grazing in the grass which had turned fall yellow. Behind the mule he could just make out a single bit plow tipped over on its side which it was dragging along as it moved from one clump of grass to the next. Jesse walked the perimeter of the field and finally found Sam sleeping under a red cedar tree. He had his arm curled around what Jesse took to be a half-empty jug. Its corn cob stopper had fallen out and lay on the grass beside it while the hooch dripped on Sam's sleeve.

It's one thing to need a pull on a jug first thing in the morning to oil your joints and get you moving in the right direction, but nobody but a two-dollar dunce took a jug out to work the fields. Sam seemed set on turning himself into a drunkard like Shakey Jim Crothers who, everybody knew, would be dead before his fortieth birthday. The word on the mountain was if the booze didn't do him in, Miz Crothers would.

Jesse kicked the soles of Sam's boots.

"Wake up, Cousin. I need you to answer a few questions."

Sam's eyes popped open and he glared at Jesse. "And if I don't answer them the way you want, are you going to break my wrist, like you done to Anse?"

"Well, I tell the truth, I hadn't given it much thought, but now you mention it, maybe I will consider doing just that, for sure. It all depends on you, Sam. Are you going to answer my question or not?"

Sam scrambled unsteadily to his feet. "What the hell do you want to know?"

Even standing two feet away, Jesse could smell the booze on Sam's breath. He took a step back. "This ain't going to be hard, Sam. You get your brains in working order for a minute and tell me how it was you all came across Jake Barker the night you near turned yourselves into murderers?"

"He were a Lebrun. There ain't no law against hanging them."

"Now that there is about the stupidest thing I heard all week. Why would you say that?"

"Anse said that Big Tom told him so."

"And you believed him? Or maybe you just wanted to, even though you knew in your heart it'd be a lie big as a hay barn. Come on, Sam, I know you ain't no college professor but you ain't entirely stupid, either."

"Anse said—"

"Just now I do not want to hear what that polecat said. His understanding of the law, the life, and the world, is as muddy as a pig's belly. All I want to know is how you all came to find Jake Baker in the first place."

Sam's face turned a bright red. Jesse guessed he was calculating his chances to duke it out or run away. Finally, he realized neither of those were even a remote possibility and he seemed to deflate.

"It were lucky, you know? It just happened. We were fixing to go get us a Lebrun 'cause Anse said they shot Solomon. So anyway, we had a pull or two on Anse's jug and—"

"Way more'n two, I think. You all was pretty likkered up when I come across you."

"Maybe. You want to hear this or do you want to play preacher?"

"Go on. I'm listening."

"We were fixing to go find us one, like I said, and here he comes riding that old broke-down horse of his and carrying an empty jug. He might have had some other gear, you know, like he might have been working on his own still and come over to our side by mistake. We didn't ask. We jumped him and had him hog-tied and a noose around his neck in, like, a minute. Then, 'fore we could finish, you came along and set him loose. Why'd you do that?"

"Why? Well, for one reason, he didn't have a blessed thing to do with shooting Solomon. At least there wasn't no evidence he did. Second, I wanted to keep you all's necks out of a noose. No matter what foolishness Anse might have told you, if you'd strung Jake up, you would go down for murder. That is, if the sheriff got wind of it. Do you realize that the folks down there in Floyd and them other towns think us up here on the mountain are not much better'n than a chicken hawk? They might go easy on one of their own, but us?…Us, they will hang every damned time whether we done the murder or not. And if the sheriff didn't send you up, the Lebruns would have. You count your blessings I stopped the five of you, friend."

Sam's brow furrowed into deep thought. The concept that there was a world other than the one he knew, and that it did not share his particular way of thinking and living, seemed to be entirely new to him and a notion he would have to turn over in his mind for a while before it sank in as real.

"Also, Sam, unless you are happy with getting a thrashing from your Pa, I think you should get that mule of yours in hand and do some plowing."

Sam turned, not too steadily, and set off across the field toward the mule. It, in turn, sensing the end to its prolonged feed, started to move away. When Sam increased his pace, so did the mule. The last Jesse saw of the both of them, the mule was at a near gallop and the plow had broken free of its hitch and sat upside down in the grass. Sam had tripped over a hummock and sat cursing at the retreating animal. He believed about half of what Sam said. Jake Baker didn't, couldn't, have just come along like Sam said. He had to be on the wrong side of the mountain for a reason.

Chapter Thirty-two

Jesse parked the Model T down the road ten yards or so and in the shade of an old oak. He wanted to be in a position where he could watch the sawmill's main gate but not be seen from the office. He hoped to catch Serena before anyone had a chance to tell her he was there. The whistle sounded and activity at the mill ground to a halt. Minutes later men carrying their lunch pails straggled through the gate. Ten minutes after that, R.G. walked over and waited until Serena slipped through and then he fastened a big brass padlock to it. He and Serena exchanged words which ended with her shaking her head. He boarded his new car and drove off. Serena headed for the road that led toward the east side of the mountain. Jesse hopped out, cranked the old Ford to life. He climbed in and overtook her before she could react to the fact he was there.

"I can offer you a ride, Serena. Hop up."

"Are you sure, Jesse? We don't seem to see eye-to-eye anymore."

"That's not necessarily a bad thing, I think. Life might become a mite dull if there wasn't no disagreements, don't you know?"

"That is your recipe for easy living? Fussing and fighting makes for a good fit?"

"That is not exactly what I am saying. I meant that good decisions come when they are hashed out first. 'Course, there has to be some respect in there on both sides."

"I will accept that for now, but I keep hold of my right to disagree with it at any time I want to in the future. In my experience, men don't always play fair when it comes to discussing a thing or two."

"If you say so."

"I do say so."

Serena clambered up into the seat beside Jesse, putting her hand on her hat expecting it to be blown off by the speed the car would achieve. She needn't have bothered. They were headed uphill and the twenty-horsepower engine with its gravity-fed fuel tank under the seat meant that Jesse might have to back it up if the fuel level happened to be too low. Either way, there wouldn't be enough wind in her face to tilt a daisy. As it happened, he'd filled the tank the day he was sent home and except for a run down to Floyd, he'd not used much gasoline. In a pinch, he had a gallon he kept as a spare strapped to the running board just in case. He could always dump it in. He thought at the time it would have been nice if Mister Ford had included a gauge of some sort that would tell him if he needed to fill up the tank. A dip stick was just fine if you weren't moving, but not of much use otherwise. He eased the clutch in. The motor coughed, caught, and they putted away. The grade was steep, but with some expert gear shifting, Jesse managed to take the car up.

Jesse had to raise his voice to be heard over the motor.

"Serena, there's a thing or two I can't get straight in my head and I need to ask you some questions."

"Questions for me? Ask away."

"What does Jake do?"

"Jake, my brother, Jake? You want to know what he does? Why is that important?"

"Well, yeah. It ain't clear to me. Does he have a job somewhere like you do? I saw your field and it ain't plowed or showing a crop, which tells me he ain't doing no farming. You all have a nice vegetable patch, but it is surrounded with flowers which makes me think you're the one tending it. So, that leaves me wondering what he does with himself all day."

"They are marigold flowers and as everybody, except maybe you know they keep the rabbits out."

"I do know that. That's not my point. I think the vegetable garden is yours, not Jake's, to plant and keep hoed. So, what does he do?"

"Why do you need to know?"

"Come on, Serena, don't get all mulish on me here. Jake like to got himself hanged back last week. One of the boys who was part of that told me Jake just wandered in on them. It was late evening. He was over on the McAdoo side. I just wondered how come he was there. It ain't natural. I figured it must have something to do with what he does, that's all."

"He hires out, Jesse. He picks up some money here and there working for farmers down in the valley. Before you ask, I can't say why he was over on the wrong side of the mountain after dark."

"Can't or won't?"

"Don't press me on this, Jesse. He's my brother. He's kin. You know about kinfolk better'n I do. Please let it go."

"Well, here's my problem with that. The boy who told me about Jake being over on the west side is not exactly deep in the brain department, if you know what I mean. The fact is, he don't have the brains of a dead possum. When he lies, everybody 'cept a newborn baby will know it. That being the case, the likelihood he'd made something up is pretty slim. He said Jake rode over on his horse big as life. He was purposeful, if you follow. His being there wasn't no chance thing. I just want to know why, is all."

"Jesse, you can put me down on the road right this very minute, you hear?"

"I aim to see you all the way home, Serena. If me asking questions is too much, I will stop. Only thing is, on Saturday, unless I get me some answers to some important questions, I will have to fight with John Henry Lebrun. Before that happens, I aim to have a chat. Jake and his near-lynching has got to come up. That could lead to some difficulties for him, maybe worse. No matter what happens there, nobody wins, everybody loses. That is an iron-clad guarantee."

Serena sat staring straight ahead and not saying a word as the little car chuffed its way upward. Jesse pulled into her yard and braked to a halt. They both sat stock still not looking at one another. Jesse turned toward her. She faced him.

"He poaches, Jesse."

"He what? There ain't no laws about hunting here. At least there's none anybody cares about."

"Not rabbits or deer, he poaches whiskey."

"Whiskey?"

"He slips into other folks whiskey stills, mostly at night, but sometimes in the daytime, if he's in need of cash money, which is mostly all the time, and poaches a jug or two. He figures people won't notice if he doesn't get too greedy. There are times when he might have anywhere from a couple of quarts to two, maybe even three gallons in a night's work."

"And then he sells it along?"

Serena nodded. "I'm sorry, Jesse, he's my brother, you know?"

"So that evening, he was over on the west side looking for a still to poach. Wait, how'd he know where to look? Somebody musta steered him. Damn...sorry...that there is dangerous, Serena. Lord love a duck, why don't you haul him down to the sawmill and put him to honest work?"

"I tried, I really did. See, he's a little short on gumption, I guess. He'll take the easy dollar every time."

"I am truly sorry to hear that. Is there anything I can do to help, talk to him, anything?"

Serena looked at Jesse, her expression as serious as death itself. Then she leaned forward and kissed him square on the lips. Before he could react, she jumped down off of the car and tripped her way across the dirt yard.

"Get off this mountain, Jesse Sutherlin, get off right now. You are too nice a person to get yourself killed over nothing."

The door of her cabin slapped shut and she was gone. A bewildered Jesse sat in his rocking Model T. The motor had started to miss. He adjusted the spark, eased the clutch, and wheeled back on the road. What had just happened?

By the time he drove the five miles of rutted road back to his own house he knew two important things he did not know before. If Solomon had caught Jake Barker poaching Big Tom's still, Jake could very well be the man who shot him. Anybody, not just a Lebrun, caught doing that would be dropped in his tracks with no questions asked, and Jake would not want to be caught. It was an idea Jesse did not want to think about.

The second thing shouldn't have been more important to him, but it was. Serena had, by God, kissed him. She must have moved closer than she'd let on. That night, it would be images her that occupied his thoughts and kept him awake, not who killed whom and what might happen Saturday at noon.

Chapter Thirty-three

Sometime back, Jesse recalled—was it really only a week?—he'd told his mother that the dark could be a time to do good as well as do bad things. Now he would find out. Something, he couldn't say what, seemed to be calling him out. He waited until the sun set and the twilight extinguished. He kissed his mother's head and looked in on Abel. There'd been no change in his brother's condition yet. Addie said she thought she saw his eyes flicker, but Jesse figured that it was more wishful thinking on her part than real. He didn't say so. Sometimes people need hope more than they need facts. This was one of those times.

He stepped into a near moonless night. He had no immediate purpose or plan. His instincts, developed in hunting and sharpened in the war, urged him to be out and away. Somewhere in that inky night someone had something to tell him. He headed toward Big Tom's house, his ears tuned tight to the night sounds. He was on patrol again and an enemy soldier, a German, might be anywhere nearby. He caught himself crouching, as if he really were in No Man's Land. He smiled at his foolishness and kept moving, as quietly as a forest floor carpeted with new fallen leaves would allow. He checked his bearings and realized he'd strayed off course and Big Tom's was way off to his left. He was about to correct his line of march when he heard voices. He froze. People were talking, more like arguing in forced whispers. It went back and forth, the whispers turned to low murmurs. One of them sounded desperate. Straight ahead. He wished he could make out words. He strained to listen. If he wanted to know what was being argued about, he'd have to move closer. If he did that, he might be discovered. He took a step. Another. Slowly, slowly. So far, so good, one step at a time. Step, pause. Step, pause. He'd moved maybe five feet when a muffled shot rang out and someone ahead of him yelped in pain. Another, louder report and that followed by the sound of feet crashing through the brush and away.

Jesse moved toward where he thought the sounds had originated. He stumbled over what he thought must be a fallen tree limb, but which turned out to be a man's leg. He lit a strike anywhere. In the flare, he saw Tommy McAdoo, Little Tom. The boy sprawled on his back. He'd been shot once in the belly and once between the eyes. Jesse stood upright. What to do? Here he was standing over the dead body of his second cousin. What would folks think? Someone had argued with Little Tom. They'd disagreed and that other person shot him once low, like maybe he had the gun hidden in his pocket, and then he must have pulled it out and finished Tommy off with a bullet square in the middle of his forehead.

Jesse turned in the direction of Big Tom's. Had he heard the report? More than likely and he'd be wondering. Only coon hunters and night light deer hunters fired guns at night. If anyone were out with their coon dogs, you'd know it. Coonhounds are a lot of things, but quiet isn't one of them. Further, the only person in this part of the country who night lighted would be Tom himself. Jesse pulled his Army automatic and fired it three times. One shot, a pause, two more in quick succession. It was the signal arranged when searching for Abel. He hoped his grandfather would remember. He heard a commotion in that direction. He repeated the gunshots. That was six out of the pistol. He only had one left. He hadn't brought the extra clip. Didn't think he'd need it.

"Hello out there. Who's shooting?" Big Tom had remembered.

"It's me, Jesse. I need some help over here. Little Tom's been shot."

"Is he hurt bad?"

"I think he's dead."

"Christ on a crutch, where you at?"

Jesse pulled the bandanna off his neck and twisted it into the tightest roll he could manage. He tied it around a stick, lit it, and waved it back and forth. As a torch, it wouldn't last long, but he figured long enough for Big Tom and whoever was with him to find their way on over.

• • ● • •

Four visibly shaken men stood around the lifeless body of Thomas Bale McAdoo, Big Tom's grandson and namesake. They were Jesse, Big Tom, Wesley, and Frank McAdoo. Jesse wondered what these men were doing this time of night at Big Tom's house but he daren't ask. Not yet. Maybe his grandfather would tell him later. There'd been a huge commotion when they carried Little Tom in. Anse burst through the door of his room, out of breath and disheveled. Nobody much noticed him. Jesse did, but dismissed it. At that moment, Anse McAdoo and his splinted wrist was the last person on Earth he wanted to waste his time thinking about. They had another killing to deal with, another one of their own and a young man too close to the center of things. Anse started to say something about the Lebruns and Big Tom wheeled on him.

"Anse McAdoo, you shut that trap of yours this very minute 'fore I put my foot in it."

"But this is just what I been saying, Grandpa. Lookit the facts. It's gotta be them Lebruns. They—"

Before he could finish his thought, Big Tom grabbed him by the collar and seat of his pants, picked him up, walked to the door, kicked it open, and tossed him out into the night. "Go home to your Momma, boy. You are as useless teats on a boar. Now git!"

Frank McAdoo rocked back and forth on his heels, his whole body shaking. Little Tom was his youngest, the last born before Frank's wife died. They said it was consumption and not the flu everybody else seemed to be dying from.

"Well, thank the Lord his Ma didn't have to see this. Who in the name of goodness done this?"

"The Lord giveth and the Lord taketh away…" Big Tom said.

"Blessed be the name of the Lord." They all mumbled in response.

It was what they always said when death came too soon and took them by surprise. Jesse must have heard the words a hundred times. It was cold comfort.

They laid Little Tom out on the bed recently vacated by Anse and sent for the undertaker.

"No police," Big Tom said. "This is something we will deal with our own selves. Jesse opened his mouth to say something, but Big Tom held up his hand. "Not now, Jesse. We all know how you feel. Trust me on this. No police."

Jesse frowned and then nodded his assent. There was something in Big Tom's voice that said, 'wait, be still,' and…'I know.' On top of that, inviting the police in would break a centuries-old precedent of ignoring the Law. Mountain folks took care of their own. That might change. Jesse hoped so. The Lebruns had called in the sheriff when Albert was murdered, hadn't they? Why, this one time, had the folks on the east side broken the unspoken tradition of avoiding the law? Or had they?

Wesley left to tell the rest of the clan. News traveled fast on the mountain. No radio, no telegraph, just word of mouth. Neighbor to neighbor, kin to kin. There were days when Jesse thought it must be done by mental telepathy. He'd seen an old faker do an act in a tent show one summer. He'd bragged that he could read folks minds. It was all a trick, but it did make you think. Did the minds of close relations sometime communicate like that? From time to time it, for sure, seemed like it.

After everything settled a bit, Big Tom motioned Jesse to join him on the porch. They sat in the dark and passed a jug.

"What were you doing out there in the dark, Jesse?"

"I don't quite know, Grandpa. Searching for answers to questions I ain't asked. I had a feeling, you could say. Not that there'd be a shooting, no, but that something was out there and I needed to go find it."

"It looks like you did."

"Maybe. I don't know."

They sat in silence for a minute, passed the jug and Big Tom lit his pipe.

"I spent an uncomfortable two hours with Garland Lebrun this afternoon, Jesse."

"That a fact? Why'd you do that?"

"You said I should jump in and do my part unraveling this business, so I did."

"What did the Kaiser have to say?"

"Who?"

"Sorry, but sometimes what we are about up here on the mountain seems more like the war in France than the Blue Ridge, that's all. On the mountain, you'd be the King of England and Garland Lebrun is Kaiser Bill."

"You can just bury that notion right this minute, thank you very much. Do you want to know what I found out or don't you?"

"I do."

"He says that none of the Lebruns had anything to do with what happened over here. He was positive about that."

"Albert said the same thing. Do you believe him?"

"I don't want to but, Lord have mercy, I do."

"Why is that?"

"Because he is a dying man and he wants to be right with the Lord 'fore he's taken. He ain't lying, Jesse." They sat in silence for a minute. "You know what that means."

"I'm afraid I do."

Chapter Thirty-four

Jesse returned home sometime after midnight. He expected he'd get a talking to from his mother. She, like mothers everywhere, would never reach the point in life where she believed her children didn't need her counsel, advice, and correcting. But he was mistaken. Addie had no words for him. She sat motionless by Abel's bed. Jesse had moved the bed from their room into the main cabin near the cookstove. The weather was turning cold and Abel didn't need being chilled half to frozen on top of his other difficulties. Addie's eyes flickered in recognition but she did not move or speak to him. Her focus stayed on her youngest child, the one, if she were to be forced to choose, dearest to her heart. She never would, of course. Jesse stood over his brother and tried to arrange some words in his mind that would serve as a prayer. One that might be acceptable to the God he'd grown up with who was generally angry over one thing or another. That made it no easy task. He realized at that moment what an advantage those Catholic boys he'd met in the service had. If they didn't have anything to say, or couldn't speak, they could just make a cross sign on their chest. It was like a prayer, like they prayed with their hands and didn't need words. He wished he could remember how it went, but he couldn't. Instead, he laid a hand on Abel's cool forehead and bowed his head. He checked his mother, who still hadn't moved or spoken, and went to bed.

Thinking about Abel did not keep him awake, nor did the shooting of Little Tom. Those things that happened should have pestered him more than a little bit, but they didn't. It was thoughts of Serena Barker and that kiss that agitated his brain. He thought, briefly, that he ought to feel guilty about that. Here he was in the tightest spot he'd been in since he tumbled into the trench full of Huns—people, cousins, kin were being shot dead, and all he could conjure up was Serena Barker's dear face and that kiss she blessed him with.

Somewhere between two and cockcrow he must have drifted off. If he slept, it was the restless kind. Whatever, he woke with a start. He could just make out his breath in the moonless dark. He swung his feet to the floor and quickly slipped them into his boots. The floor was like ice, his boots only slightly less so. He pulled his blanket close around his shoulders and silently thanked the U.S. Army for providing him with one twice as thick as the ones he grew up with and now lay folded and put away for another day, another time.

What had stirred him awake? He stood, considered a trip in the dark to the privy, and then he heard it...a moan? Something. Jesse made his way out into the big room. His mother sat exactly where he'd left her. Now her head lolled to one side and mouth open, she snored gently. She would pay for this vigil with a cow-sized crick in her neck in the morning. It was Abel who drew his attention. Abel's eyes were open and staring at the ceiling. It was as if he could see straight through the roof to the stars above. It scared Jesse a bit, that stare did. He leaned closer.

"Abel, you with us?"

No reply.

"Abel, who did this to you?"

"Sumbitch."

"What?"

"Sumbitch."

"What son of a bitch did it?"

"Him, din see 'im."

Abel's eyelids fluttered shut.

"Abel, who hit you?"

Nothing.

Addie stirred. "That you Jesse?"

"It's me. Abel woke up there for a minute. He said some words and dropped off again."

"Why didn't you wake me?"

"It took up only maybe a second, Ma. I came out here, something woke me, I guess, and I happened to look at Abel. His eyes was wide open, scary like. Then, they slid over and he like to look at me. Well, I asked him if he was here, you know, awake? He didn't say a word. Then I asked who it was that put him in this fix."

"He answered!"

"Yep."

"What'd he say?"

"He said son of a bitch."

"He said what? I never taught him to talk like that. It must have been his Pa done that."

"Ma..."

"Well, I didn't. What else? Did he say anything else?"

"Not really. I think he tried to tell me he didn't see who hit him."

"That's all?"

"That's all."

Addie slumped back in her rocker. "It ain't much, but it's something. It is, ain't it?"

"Yessum, it is. It means his brain ain't dead and soon enough he'll come back to us."

"Well, praise the Lord for that. I'll fix us a pot and maybe I can find something to eat. It's what you do when good news comes in the front door."

• • ● • •

Garland Lebrun told Big Tom that no Lebruns were involved in Solomon's shooting and none of them for sure killed Albert Lebrun either. In the light of this last killing, that assertion begged at least two questions: who killed Little Tom and how did one define being a Lebrun? Clan lines got fuzzy when you got out on the edges. Jesse was a McAdoo for sure because he was in a straight line from his grandpa and that line stretched clear back to the Flood, for all he knew, but out on the perimeter...out there were the Billingsleys, for example. Were they McAdoos? Their connection was more about geography than blood. Sure there was a marriage in there somewhere, hardly anybody remembered where or when, but it was a pretty thin connection. Were the Barkers really Lebruns? Serena said they were because of a cousin connection or something, but there again, how tight was it? More important, would a dying Garland Lebrun who, while straightening out his record with the Lord, also narrow the definition to keep Lebruns clean and clear from the murders? Blood made for an odd kind of loyalty.

In the war, men were bound by a different kind of blood relationship—spilled blood. Those men he fought with, some of whose names he could hardly pronounce, he'd bled for them. He'd put his life on the line for them and they weren't McAdoos. They weren't even family, not even close. But he'd have died for them. Now? Sweet Jesus, well, now he might have to fight John Henry Lebrun and maybe die. And he was to do that for the honor of the McAdoos? He should die for Anse and the idiot Sam Knox and Little Tom and the two Crowther boys, who'd come close to stringing up Jake Baker? How could that have anything to do with honor?

Jesse had no doubt about the connection between this last killing and the first. He couldn't have told you what that connection was, but he had no doubts about there being one. The thoughts rattled around in his head like seeds in a dried-up gourd. He found a place to sit and tried to get his brain to think in a straight line. If he were a policeman, how would he go about making the connection? That was a poser. Nothing in his growing up or his time as a soldier prepared him for the kind of thinking needed to unravel a puzzle this messy. It was like when your fishing line got snarled. After an hour of picking at the tangle, you were mighty tempted to just go at it with a knife. That was pretty much what the folks on the mountain did. See a knotty problem; don't bother to sort it out. Can't be done. Instead, just point a finger at them other people and accuse them for making it. McAdoos would naturally holler, "Lebrun." Lebruns would yell back, "McAdoo." Nobody tried to pick it apart. Just hack at it with a knife.

He sat on the porch step, still cocooned in his Army blanket, and watched the sun wrench itself free of the mountain to the east and rise up to splash new light on his part of the world. He thought that, by God, he was going to pick the thing apart if it took 'til Saturday. If he hadn't untangled it by then, well, whether he liked it or not, there'd have to be the knife after all.

Chapter Thirty-five

Jesse hadn't moved from the porch step when Serena hove into view. Her long legs propelled her from the road and into the yard. Jesse was embarrassed; he still had on only his long johns and boots. The Army blanket was the only thing between him and cause for alarm in the woman department. He hugged the brown blanket closer and tried to get to his feet and still stay covered.

"You do not look like a man who is contemplating a death sentence." She'd stopped a way off, apparently relishing the difficulty he'd put himself in. "Don't get up on my account."

Jesse lowered himself back down to the porch step.

"You are a long way from your hearth and home, Serena Barker, and in enemy territory, if I hear rightly. I don't believe you come over here for a social call. Is there something wrong at the mill…at home?"

"Nope, none of those things. Your lawyer friend telephoned the mill yesterday late and left you an important message."

"He did? That was mighty nice of him. Would you be able to repeat it to me?"

She took a step or two closer. Jesse pulled the blanket tighter. She grinned at his predicament. "I could, for sure. I am not sure I should, though."

"Because?"

"I don't know if I can trust communicating with a man who sits around in his drawers and hob-nobs with lawyers."

"Which is it, the drawers or the lawyers?"

"Well there you go again, making poetry."

"It is always a pleasure to provide entertainment to the secretarial corps. The message?"

"Mister Nicholas Bradford, Esquire, says to inform you, and here I repeat his words exact, 'the deal is done. You need to get down here'…that'd be Floyd, I reckon…'and sign some papers.' That is the message and with that, I will say goodbye."

Serena turned and took a step, turned back again.

"Jesse—"

"Little Tom McAdoo was shot last night, Serena. Who could have done that, you think?"

"Another dead man. There ain't no end, is there?"

"I need some help here, Serena. You were about to tell me again to run. I would if I could, but now I can't."

She walked closer, no longer mindful or caring of his relative state of undress. "I'll go with you, Jesse. You said you'd leave if I went. Well, I will go with you, if you want me to."

"Because you don't want me dead and will sacrifice yourself for a good Christian end, or because of something else?"

"Don't do that, Jesse. It's not fair."

"I won't. Here's the problem. A day ago, I would have jumped at the offer. You know that. To die for some old-fashioned notion about family and honor didn't appeal to me then, and not now either, but things has got out of hand. There is a murderer loose on this mountain. I am about convinced it don't have a blessed thing to do with the Lebruns or McAdoos. As long as he's loose, nobody is safe. Fact is, if there is a pattern here, and I'm inclined to think there is, that could include you. I will give you your own advice back, Serena, go away. Go away at least until this business is over."

"I can't do that, Jesse, any more than you can."

"Then we are in this together, whether we like it or not."

"I'm not complaining."

They looked at each other long and hard. Serena's eyes seemed sort of shiny. She shook her head, adjusted her little straw bonnet and started back down the way she'd come.

"A whole lot of folks care about you, Jesse Sutherlin, so you be careful, you hear?"

"Would you happen to be one of them folks?"

She didn't answer.

• • ● • •

Jesse parked against the boardwalk in front of Bradford's office. He thought he spied a familiar face ten yards farther down next to a dusty Essex. He took a stroll toward the car and, sure enough, it had the writing on the door. Sam Schwartz had returned to Floyd. The same stepped out of his car and waved.

"So, Mister Jesse, where is your hat?"

"I am giving it a well-deserved rest today, Mister Schwartz. What brings you and your haberdashery back to Floyd?"

"Ah, you should ask. Well first, I am for thanking you. I took your good advice and drove to Picketsville. Right on the nose, you were about that town. They do not have anything like a good place for men's clothes and accessories. They did have a store for rent. So now I am settled there. I came down to Floyd to see Gottlieb. He has merchandise he wishes to dispose of. He is unhappy with his new name, it seems. He wants to trade as Gottlieb, not Lord and Lovett. He is planning on resettling in a bigger town where he can start over as Gottlieb. You can make your name sound like something else, but He knows."

"He?"

"The Lord. Never try to fool Him, Mister Sutherlin. Take some advice."

"I hear you, Mister Schwartz, and good luck up there in Picketsville."

"And to you, too, in the sawing of wood."

Jesse retraced his steps to Bradford's door. Miss Primrose gave him a look that would curdle cream and banged on a button mounted in a box on her desk. Somewhere in the distance he heard a bell ringing, six bursts, a pause and four more. Was it a code so Bradford would know who just came in? Six and four…

How you gon-na keep 'em…down on the farm?

A beaming Nicholas Bradford popped out of his office.

"Come right on in, Jesse. We have us some papers to sign and get you on your way to your first million, by Godfrey."

The paperwork was simple. Jesse signed a document claiming the abandoned property, a deed transfer, and he became the owner of The Oaks, which turned out to be more like twelve acres, not ten. With the deed came a plat map showing the property lines and the markers. If he wasn't mistaken, Charlie Bascomb was planting on one corner of Jesse's new holdings. Jesse had to pay Bradford a dollar for the land to make it official. Then he had to borrow it back because it was the last bit of cash he had. Payday would be tomorrow, but a trip to the mill might not be something he'd do. Maybe Serena could bring him his pay envelope.

Bradford leaned back in his big oak swivel chair. "Well, Jesse, what happens next?"

Jesse told him of the situation he found himself in, the latest killing and what he might have to do on Saturday.

"I have not heard a word you've said, Jesse. If anybody asks, you never told me this."

"I didn't? Why didn't I?"

"Because, if I heard you right, and mind you, I didn't hear anything, you all have trampled your way across at least three statutes which could get you fined or jailed and you are about to crash into another."

"I guess not reporting a murder is one of them. I ain't so sure about the rest."

"I would elaborate, but as I said, I haven't heard a word. Well, except you should be aware that dueling is also against the law. What you plan to do with that other young man up on the mountain constitutes a duel, clear and simple, and it is against the law. That is to say you might have one and not suffer any consequence except someone is killed. Then, honor or not, it's considered murder.'

"Up on the mountain, there is not a whole lot of worry about what the Law says about most things, Mister Bradford."

"So they say. So they say. Do you want me to send a policeman up on the mountain to arrest you two when you start? That way you won't get yourself killed and won't lose face either."

Jesse grinned. "I think that would be a first rate idea, Mister Bradford, Esquire. I ain't the least bit worried about losing face, if I understand what that means, but a state policeman could come in mighty handy. Tell him this Saturday noon he should get himself up to the top of the mountain and then follow the path down into the meadow on the south side. It would be best if he were not in uniform, though. The folks up there would rather have the French disease than have a policeman inside a mile of them. He should do his best to look like he belongs. The Lebruns will think he's McAdoo and them will think the opposite. Yes, sir, that will be just dandy."

"You're serious?"

"I am. There is one other thing I need you to do."

"Name it."

"I need a will. Just in case your policeman don't come or don't act in time or I can't put an end to the foolishness without getting myself killed, which is the plan, by the way. Having him stop us is the last resort. You and him need to know that people up there are getting techey. It's like a powder keg, Mister Bradford. It won't take much to set her off. Like I said, the whole mountain could blow at any minute."

Chapter Thirty-six

When he returned home, he found his mother and Abel on the porch. Somehow she'd managed to get him bundled up and in a chair. He looked a whole lot better. Maybe that came from being out in the sunlight, or maybe he had made some progress.

"Well, Abel, you're up and about. You feeling perky? Can you tell me what happened to you?"

"He ain't spoke much, Jesse. He give a grunt or two when I was getting him dressed and hauled him out here. Nothing else." Addie turned to Abel and barked at her son. "You ain't said a thing, has you, Abel?"

"Ma, he ain't sitting over in the next county, you know."

"What?"

"You don't have to yell at him. He ain't deaf, you know. He just has trouble in the answering. Ain't that right, Abel?"

A ghost of a smile flickered across Abel's face.

"There, you see, he ain't deaf. So just chat with a normal voice is all."

"Well, how in the world will I know he's a hearing me?"

"Abel, can you blink?"

Abel blinked one eye, a wink.

"I reckon that will have to do. Are you hungry?"

Wink.

"Ma, why don't you heat up that broth left over from cooking the chicken. Put some cornbread in it and make mush. I expect Abel can manage that. What do you say, Abel?"

Wink.

"There you go. So, Abel, you said some son of a bitch done you in, that right?"

Wink.

"You can stop talking that trash right this very minute, you hear?"

"Sorry, Ma. I'm just trying to keep him on track. But you can't say who. That right?"

Wink. Smile.

"Did he say anything to you? Oh shoot. We have to figure out how to tell a yes, from a no. Okay. Abel, one blink for yes, two for no. Okay?"

Wink.

"So, a voice?"

Wink, wink.

"Shoot."

Addie returned with a bowl of mush. "You leave him be for a while. I think he wants to eat now. You do, don't you, son?"

Wink.

The evening wore on to nightfall. Abel ate nearly all of the broth/cornbread mix. His winking turned to blinking. "He's using both his eyes," Addie sounded like Abel had just discovered Radium. An hour after sundown, Abel's eyes began to flutter.

"What's he trying to say?"

"Ma, that ain't him trying to talk. I think he's falling asleep. All his trying to answer questions has wore him out. You're tuckered, ain't you Abel?"

Blink.

"You ready to lie down again?"

Blink.

"Got both eyes working now. There you go. Here, I'll help you get him back to bed. It's probably a good thing if we all turned in. You ain't had a real night's sleep for days, Ma."

"I am just fine."

"And I am the King of England. You go to bed."

"Jesse, about Saturday…"

"You just put that out of your mind, you hear? I didn't make it all through the war just to come home and have some pup stick a knife in me, did I?"

"But—"

"No buts, Ma. Go lie down. Tomorrow you likely are going to be busted keeping up with Abel. You need to get your sleep."

They managed to settle Abel in the bed near the stove. The fire was banked so it would spring to life in the morning with a few sticks of kindling. Addie went off to bed. Jesse checked on both of them a half hour later and they both slept like the dead. He blew out the lantern and found his way to bed as well. He did not, however, drop off to sleep. He had tomorrow, Friday, to finish this business or he'd need to decide what to do on Saturday. He couldn't see any good news looming up on his horizon.

• • ● • •

The sun leaked through his window. He must have dropped off to sleep. That was the thing about sleep: you only remembered the times you were awake. He could have sworn he hadn't slept at all, but here he was, surprised by the sunlight. He shuffled out into the main room. Abel had managed to sit up in his bed. He smiled at the sight of his brother.

"Hey there, Abel. You are looking pretty perky this morning. What you got to say for yourself?"

"Unh…Sorr…ee."

"You spoke another word. Ma. Where's Ma at? She needs to hear this. Ma!"

A sleepy and unsteady Addie walked in. "Land sakes, what time is it? I must have slept in. I ain't been this late rousing in thirty years. What are you hollering about, Jesse?"

"He talked again. Something new."

Who talked?"

"Who do you think? Abel did."

"No."

"He did. Abel, say hi to your Ma."

"Mmmmmmm."

"Well. That's close enough for now. Ma, Abel needs breakfast. Don't you?"

"Jez…?"

"Yeah, what Abel?"

"Sorry."

"Sorry about what?"

"Nnn…node."

"What? You mean the note you got that was meant for me. Hey, I'm the one who should be sorry. I should have been here, not running all over creation trying to make me some money."

"What you mean, make yourself some money? What are you up to, Jesse? It better not be no swindle."

"Relax, Ma. You know me better'n that. I am only going to sell some timber rights on some land I got ahold of. It is all on the square, I promise. Hey, Abel, what do you think? You and me in the timber business?"

Addie pulled a face. "Well, I don't like it."

"What don't you like, Ma?"

"Easy money is always got a problem stuck on it like a pig's tail, all crookedy."

"I promise you, this is four square, straight up honest,"

"Humph. Abel, you ready to eat?"

"Jez, din mean to get inna way."

"Hush that talk up right now. You did what you thought you had to do. I am proud of you. You want to make up for anything, you get your lazy rear end up out of that bed and help me sort out the mess we got ourselves into."

Abel smiled, stronger than the night before, and some life seemed to come into his eyes.

"I believe the boy is going to make it, Ma. I really do."

"You get yourself out of the way and let me stir up the fire and cook us up some breakfast. Hand me that side of bacon. You go grind us up some coffee beans and get the jug down off the shelf. Abel is in need of a pick-me-up, ain't you, Abel?"

• • ● • •

Jesse spent the morning visiting and revisiting the places where people had been killed or nearly so. He particularly wanted to go over the ground where Jake had been nearly hanged. Something about that night gnawed at him and he couldn't figure out why. Sam Knox told him Jake had an empty jug when they caught him. That made sense since Serena confessed that her brother poached hooch. But one jug? This far over on the west side of the mountain and he only had one? Anse, Sam, Little Tom, and the two Crother boys were likkered up that night. Where did they get ahold of all that drinking whiskey? Everybody knew those boys couldn't raise two bits between the five of them. Where'd they come up with two dollars for a jug, maybe four for two? All this made you think that they were into something more than their usual mischief before they took on Jake. Unless...unless Jake stashed his jugs between poaching and collected them after he got done. That would be the safe thing to do. If he got caught with one, who'd say anything? But if he was lugging four or five, maybe more.... that'd be enough evidence to get himself shot. If those boys had come across his stash...or...Or they could be trading hooch for showing him the locations of the McAdoo stills. Hadn't he found Sam Knox halfway to a liquid hell with a jug when he went to talk to him? He needed to have another talk with Sam. He needed to find out everything they were up to that night and Sam needed to know, if he already didn't already, that if Little Tom could be killed for what he knew, so could Sam. That went for the Crother boys, too.

Chapter Thirty-seven

Jesse had some hard looks sent his way when he went over to the east side to look at where Albert Lebrun died. No matter what he said or what the court decided, folks still reckoned he was the man who had put a knife in Albert. The only reason someone didn't shoot him on the spot this very minute was because John Henry Lebrun had put in a prior claim to do him in and the rest of that clan was willing to honor it. If John Henry didn't get it done, another Lebrun or two would step up and that would go on, one after another until Jesse ended up in a grave somewhere. There would be no end to it until one of two things happened—everybody died or he found a way to set them all off on a different course.

Jesse did not linger long at the spot. He inspected the place where Albert fell, turned halfway around and stared in the bushes. He turned back and took four steps and spent a minute kicking at the ground with his toe and then took himself back to the friendly side of the mountain. He breathed a whole lot easier when he could see Big Tom's place through the trees.

In the daylight, the area where Little Tom had been shot seemed noticeably different. It had been disturbed the most. That surprised Jesse. You would have thought that the area where Albert died would have been disturbed the most. After all, the Lebruns had called in the police. Sheriff Franklin and his deputies would have bumbled around and trampled all over it. Yet, here, where only Jesse and the McAdoos had been, it looked like a pair of mountain lions had fought over who got to mate with the lady cat. It looked like somebody might have come out here and deliberately scuffed his feet through the leaves to scramble any attempt to reconstruct what happened.

If he'd a mind to destroy evidence, he came up short on his exit. Jesse easily picked up the path the killer took when he ran off. In the pitch black that night was, with hardly any moon and all, a person would have the Devil's own time not leaving a trail behind him when he went crashing through the forest. Sure enough, Jesse didn't have to be one of the local Cherokee Indian guides that the swells from the city hired to show them where the deer were hiding to follow the bent and broken branches on bushes and trees, shuffled leaves, and all the other signs that someone came through here in a hurry. Whoever pulled the gun on Little Tom had headed along here straight east 'til he hit a path. It happened to be one of the well-used and walked-on by a lot of folks because it connected the two sides of the mountain. He could only assume the killer kept heading east once he got to that point. It wasn't a certainty, but a reasonable guess.

Walking the ground around Big Tom's still didn't turn up anything new. Jesse headed home.

Addie made fresh pone and brought a jug of buttermilk up from the spring where she kept the few items that would spoil in the heat. With winter coming, putting crocks in the spring wouldn't be necessary much longer. Jesse's Pa had built his wife a little box attached to the back wall that had a hinged door inside and out. All you had to do, if you wanted a jug of cream or something, was to open the little door and bring it in. You didn't even have to put your shoes on or nothing. Once in a great while, the heat from the house wasn't enough to keep the contents from freezing, but that didn't happen too often.

Abel sat at the table with them. He didn't say much and Jesse didn't press him. His appetite had returned and he managed to wolf down as much by himself as Jesse and his mother combined. Addie poured coffee and they all pushed back.

"Why'd they hit me, Jesse? Were they mad 'cause I come in your place?"

"It wasn't that, Abel. They tried to kill you 'cause they thought you were me."

"They did? How'd they come by that? I don't look nothing like you."

"Your back was to them. Probably the sun was in their eyes, that time of day, but mostly, I think it was because you were wearing one of my Army coats that Ma put on you. I suppose they saw that and jumped straight to the notion that the person standing on the creekbank was me. I reckon there's a jaw or two dropped when I turned up alive the next day. "

"Holy Ned. Why'd they want to kill you? Wait a durn minute, you think a Lebrun come after you because you stabbed Albert Lebrun and they wanted to even it up?"

"Abel, an ocean or two has flowed under that bridge since you dropped off on your long nap. It might have been one of them, I ain't saying it weren't, but Lebruns as the Devil's Disciples is currently off the table."

"What?"

"A right smart lot of things happened lately. Little Tom's been killed. We don't know by who or why—"

"No! He was the one who give me the note for you. Is that why he's dead?"

"Wait. Little Tom brought the note? Did he say where he got it?"

"I don't remember exactly. I think he said one of the little kids over on the other side give it to him. Hey, maybe it was one of them whose footprints we saw."

"Yeah, maybe. But that don't explain why he's dead."

"Well, shoot, I know why. He was the one who delivered a note that could of pointed out who killed Solomon."

"No, that won't wash, Abel. Like I said, things has moved mighty fast here lately. Big Tom has met with Garland Lebrun and they might have come to an understanding of sorts."

"No, you're pulling my leg. He is, ain't he, Ma?"

"It ain't my place to say. It don't seem even natural, but that is what they're saying."

"It's a true fact, brother. Also, me and John Henry didn't have our set-to…not yet, anyway. It's been crazy busy around here lately."

"I don't understand. You didn't kill Albert like you said in the courthouse you didn't?"

"That's right. I am a great disappointment to the McAdoos generally, but no, I did not send Albert Lebrun to a cold and lonely grave. Because of that, the problem comes up, if I didn't, who did? Nobody over here is claiming it and, for sure, nobody over there is, either."

Abel slumped in his chair, his face darkened by a frown. "Little Tom is dead?"

"Yep. Someone shot him twice not two hundred yards from our front door."

Addie patted her son on the wrist. "Abel, honey, you got enough to think about without worrying yourself with all this mess. You brother has got it in hand, ain't you, Jesse? You'll see. Everything is going to be alright. Ain't that so?"

Jesse nodded and forced a smile and wished it were so. Unfortunately, as much as he tried, he didn't see a rosy end to this particular story. He wished he could at least put one or two of the puzzle pieces together. That's how it is with jigsaw puzzles. You had to get something started before anything looked like it was supposed to. He excused himself and wandered into his bedroom. Unless he had himself a miracle, tomorrow he would go up against John Henry. Would the state policeman show? Was Bradford having him on about that? If he did show up, what would he do? What could he do? Would he be brave enough to step in between a few dozen armed and angry Lebruns and McAdoos and try to stop it? If he had the sense of a bumble bee he wouldn't. He wouldn't last ten seconds if he did.

Jesse pulled the box of his old Army equipment out from under his bed. One of the Limeys he'd run into showed him his Dayfield Shield, a little vest that had metal plates sewed in it. Jesse wished he'd managed to talk the Englishman out of it when he'd had a chance. He heard later that the Brit was killed anyway when a bullet slid in between the plates. Bad luck, that was. He grabbed a few items, his sharpening stone, and leather strop and walked into the woods. Tomorrow was coming and there was nothing he could do about it except be prepared. He took a swipe at a sapling and severed its spindly trunk in one clean cut. It toppled gently into the leaves and rolled a foot or two away. He paused and turned back to stare at the fallen tree, then smiled, and resumed his walking. Things could be worse. Not much, but some.

Chapter Thirty-eight

The view from the top of Buffalo Mountain is considered one of the better if not the best in that corner of Virginia. Jesse might have agreed, but the mountain was his home and the view, as with everything else there, just an everyday thing. In any case, it was the last thing on his mind that evening. He had come to reconnoiter. Only a fool fought on ground he didn't know intimately. Too many generals raised up in places like Kansas or Ohio found that out to their sorrow in the war. The funny thing about it; you'd have thought the French would have had a better handle on the ground than they did. Apparently the success in Verdun convinced them they didn't need to do any more scouting. Anyway, the one piece of strategy Jesse had learned in that war that he felt sure would help him in this one had to do with knowing the ground. In any fight, whether it involved clubs or howitzers, the person who held the high ground started with an important advantage.

He worked his way down to the creekbed he'd mentioned to Jake as the place he would meet John Henry. A trickle of water kept the bed damp and muddy. He climbed out of the creek and worked his way along its course. He searched for an area that was nearly flat. The high ground he wanted to keep at his back. That way, if he needed to, he could take it by retreating. John Henry would be so happy to see him back away, that he wouldn't notice he'd lost that advantage. Jesse positioned himself in the spot he'd choose to stand the next day. He turned completely around, memorizing every feature of the land in the full three hundred and sixty degrees. Satisfied he'd done all he could, he trudged back up to the summit. The evening was fast upon him and the light was fading. He didn't see the figure at the top until he'd nearly reached it. He didn't realize it was Serena until he stood in front of her.

"What are you doing here, Serena?"

"Well, that ain't much of a greeting. Where'd you lose your manners, Jesse?"

"There's plenty of those who'll tell you I never had any. I ask again, why are you here?"

"Unless you happen to be the owner of this particular piece of the mountain, it's none of your business where I am or aim to be."

"As you wish. I can see a chance for a polite social call is not going to happen."

They stood side by side looking off to the west and the setting sun not saying a word.

"Temperature is dropping, Jesse. You could catch your death up here."

"I don't believe you just said that."

"What? Why? Oh, no I didn't mean it that way. I'm sorry."

"I have this greatcoat the Army give me. I won't freeze anytime soon. I can't say the same for that flimsy shawl you're hiding yourself in."

"I am just fine and dandy right like I am."

"If you say so."

"I do say so."

"Okay. How'd you find me?"

"Maybe I just came up here to enjoy the view."

"Maybe. In the freezing cold, you came to see the view you been looking at your whole life. How, Serena?"

"Your Ma said you were headed up here. She wasn't too pleased about that or me asking, but she told me anyway."

Jesse shrugged on the coat and pulled it close around his body. "They made the coats some of the officers wore double-breasted, like this one here."

Serena tried and failed to suppress a bout of shivering. "Well that is very interesting to know, I'm sure."

They stood unmoving and in silence. The last of the sun disappeared behind the next mountain. The twilight deepened. Serena shivered again.

"There is room for two in this old coat, if you're interested." Jesse opened the coat and Serena folded herself in and put her arms around him. "Holy Ned, you are an iceberg, girl."

"You shut your mouth. I ain't any such thing."

"Maybe not in your heart, you ain't, but your whole body, including your clothes, is like you been sled-riding in your nightgown."

"My nightgown is definitely none of your business, Mister Sutherlin."

"Nope, not yet."

"Not yet? Not ever. By—"

Serena did not finish her thought because Jesse planted a kiss on her lips. He felt her stiffen and then relax. He kept on kissing her until she broke free.

"What do you think you are doing, Jesse Sutherlin?"

"Well, I thought that was kinda obvious, Serena Barker."

"We can't..."

"We can. Listen, Serena, I need to say some words right now and I need you to listen to them all the way to the end. If what you hear means you never want to see me again, okay, but hear me out."

"If you are going to preach me a sermon about duty and honor, about being a man and all that foolishness, I will not listen. Men has spent centuries talking that talk and then going off to war and getting themselves killed, or maimed, or made crazy like your cousin Solomon. And what for? Nothing. When enough of you is dead, what's left over staggers home and sits around and talks about glory. Well, I don't want to hear it, Jesse."

"Serena, I—"

"And who has to pick up all the pieces? Who has to patch you up when you all come limping home? And who is left behind to tend the children and the farm while you all are off being stupid and honorable? It'd be us, is who. It's us women. We are the ones who hold the world together while you all march off to glorious war. And then you think we haven't earned the right to vote?"

"Are you all done?"

"Maybe."

"Serena, I will tell you what I told my Ma back a while. I didn't spend all those months in the trenches, fighting Germans, tumbling into trenches full of them in the dark and crawling out bloody but alive, just to come back here to be done in by an upstart boy who's developed a brain cramp. I cannot tell you what will happen here tomorrow, but honor and bravery will not be the featured item. I do not have anything to prove. You know that."

"But then why?"

"Hear me out. I have a brother, you know. He has a sweet disposition and left to his own self, he wouldn't step on a bug. But in this crazy divided piece of civilization we have created on the mountain, Lord only knows how many hundred years ago, he thinks it's his duty to gun down anybody named or connected to Lebrun who so much as looks cross-eyed at him. You got people over on your side who feel the same. It don't make sense. You can't find a reason for it, but there it is. It is like we're all raised up angry and can't see straight. It's got to stop. Solomon, Albert, Little Tom, and Abel almost…who's next? That is why I will be here on this meadow tomorrow, not for glory, or honor, or out of loyalty to a situation that is a hundred years behind the times. I aim, one way or another, to put an end to it. That, or die trying."

"Jesse…"

"Shhh…Let me finish. I made me a will, Serena, just in case I fail at this. The title to The Oaks and all the money the timber rights might bring in goes to you. I expect that you will see that my Ma is took care of and—"

Serena stopped him with a kiss of her own. Several, in fact.

"We should go," Jesse said after five or maybe more like ten minutes slid by.

"Why?" Serena sounded a little out of breath. "You said so yourself, this coat is plenty big enough for two."

"Well, yeah."

"So, would that be standing up only, or do you think it might work as good if we were to sit down?"

"Better maybe. You are a wicked woman. Okay, there ain't but one way to find out."

"Do you suppose we could get off these rocks and onto some grass first?"

Chapter Thirty-nine

The night sky was flooded with stars. Only a quarter moon competed with them for attention. Time seemed to stop for them. Finally, Serena stirred and sat upright.

"What time has it got to be?"

Jesse checked the radium dial of his watch. "Going on two."

"This is once in my life I am happy I do not have parents at home. I would have dogs out hunting for me and when they found me, someone would show up at your doorstep with a shotgun. What have we done here, Jesse?"

"I believe we have made a commitment to each other."

"A what? What we did is hardly called making a commitment."

"What would you call it?"

"Oh, my golly. What comes next?"

"Right now, I think I should walk you straight home. Come Sunday, you and me will have a word with the preacher about getting married. After that, well there is some decisions to be made about living arrangements and such."

"You really want to marry me? This ain't some idea you have about 'making an honest woman out of me,' is it? Because if it is, I ain't having it."

"It is about something I been thinking about since before I went to France. I think I must have been in love with you since I was old enough to know there was a difference between girls and boys."

"Is that true?"

"It is. Swear on my daddy's grave."

"Mercy. How'd you know?"

"It just come to me. So, will you marry me?"

In the starlight, Jesse could just make out a smile. The she sat up and recited:

How do I love thee? Let me count the ways.
I love thee to the depth and breadth and height
My soul can reach, when feeling out of sight
For the ends of being and ideal grace.
I love thee to the level of every day's
Most quiet need, by sun and candle-light.

"That's that Portuguese poem."

"It is, hush up."

I love thee freely, as men strive for right.
I love thee purely, as they turn from praise.
I love thee with the passion put to use"

"You won't get no argument from me."

"Be still, or I take it all back."

"Oops."

In my old griefs, and with my childhood's faith.
I love thee with a love I seemed to lose
With my lost saints. I love thee with the breath,
Smiles, tears, of all my life; and, if God choose,
I shall but love thee better after death.

She took a breath. "Jesse Sutherlin, I will marry you, I will, but there is a one condition."

"Oh, oh. What's that? I can't not show tomorrow."

"I know that now. That's not it. I will marry you but you have to survive tomorrow. You can't get yourself killed, you hear me?"

"Staying alive is definitely my plan, more now than ever."

"No, let's get married first. At least I'll have that if things don't work out."

"Except for saying the words in front of a preacher, I reckon we already are."

"The preacher and saying words don't seem so needed now. Just in case, come here and let's make it for sure."

• • ● • •

For once, Jesse's mother wasn't waiting for him to come home. That had to be considered a mercy. He looked in on her. She slept peacefully. The stove seemed to have gone cold and he added some kindling. The fire caught and he added a few sticks. A few minutes later, he had enough heat to set the pot with the leftover dinner coffee boiling. He poured a cup and retreated to the table to drink and think over the last week. Whatever happened tomorrow, his life and that of many others would be forever changed. Not for the first time he wondered if that might not be the good thing he imagined. Loving Serena would, of course, but the rest? What right had he, when had God Almighty anointed him, to judge his family, his friends, or his enemies?

People said he should just run. Serena would happily go with him now. Could he run away from what had happened to Abel? From what happened to three men from the mountain who'd played together as children? They were dead and maybe there'd be more to come. Whatever was driving this probably wouldn't be satisfied with three. Someone wanted him dead, too. Did he dare turn his back on that?

"What are you doing up this time of night? If I didn't know you better, I'd say you was hoping to kill yourself before John Henry Lebrun has his chance to do it."

Addie stood in the doorway of the room she and her late husband had slept in for the twenty-five years of their marriage and in which she now slept alone. Jesse's father had built the room as an add-on to the cabin when their firstborn arrived. He'd added clapboards to the sides after Jesse's birth and a porch after Abel's.

"Why ain't you asleep yourself?"

"How can a body sleep with you rattling pot and pans around?"

"Sorry, I tried to be quiet. There's a tad more coffee in the pot if you want."

"Naw, it will keep me awake. 'Course, it ain't that far to sun-up. Maybe I will get me an early start."

Jesse poured out a cup from the pot, inspected its interior and took it to the sink to rinse out.

"Tell me you ain't going through with that meeting tomorrow, well, today, for a fact."

Jesse folded his hands around his coffee mug. How to answer? He knew there were no words, nothing he could say, that would make any sense to his mother. Her only instinct was to keep him alive. The notion of cowardice or pride occupied an unsteady perch in her mind. Keeping her children safe and alive pushed everything else to the back.

"Ma, it won't be what you think."

"What does that mean? Either you get on up the mountain and take on that Lebrun boy, or you don't. He will either kill you or you will kill him. What else can happen? Has they made up new rules on fighting? You going to use wooden knives, wear knight armor? What?"

"It means that none of those things will or even have to happen. I will find a way to make him talk to me. I will make the two sides of the mountain sit down and talk."

"And then, I reckon, you will smack the dirt with a stick and make the Red Sea part, or bring down fire from heaven, or cause a plague of locusts, and pigs will fly. When did you decide to become a miracle worker?"

"It won't be a miracle. Listen, you know I ain't one to brag, but do you know what I did to get that medal? You don't 'cause I never told anyone. I come out of that German trench alive, and six of them didn't. How I ended up in there is a story for another day, but there I was. There was a moment, you know, like time was froze, like nobody moved and it just stood still. In that little second, I knew."

"Knew what?"

"I knew that I was not going to die that night, that the Lord was going to deliver me out of that place like he done with Daniel from the lion's den. Some others were going to their maker, but not me. It was as clear as one of them goblet things the rich folk drink their wine from, or maybe a mountain spring, all shiny bright. Whatever, I just knew that it was not my time to go. Well, that moment passed and we went at each other. A rifle and a bayonet are pretty useless when you're all jammed in together. You squeeze off a shot and hope to hit somebody, take a stab at one and then it's trench knives, or clubs, or anything heavy you can lay your hands on. The point is, what I did in that trench wasn't glorious and it weren't honorable. It was messy, and dirty, and bloody, but I was right. I was banged up some, did my share of bleeding, but that night, it was like I had on the full armor of God, like the Book says, and I was not going to die and I didn't. Six German soldiers figured they had me and they ended up being the dead ones. The rest of them put their hands in the air and surrendered. Ma, I ain't proud of that. I was raised up on this mountain and it is a hard place where shooting someone over a disagreement is part of the way we live, but killing ain't something I ever got used to. I see them German boys' dead faces in my dreams most every night. I didn't know them men. They didn't know me. We weren't even angry at each other as far as I know. We just got put in a place where our only choice was to kill or be killed. It didn't make sense then and it don't now. That's how it is with us and the Lebruns. I am just plain tired of it all. And, for what it's worth, I got that feeling…I am not going to die on top of this mountain tomorrow."

"Woo, I think you been talking to that Barker girl and she's got your brains scrambled. I must have told you a hundred times, you can't trust a Lebrun."

"There you go. You are right, you told me that from the time I was a tadpole, clear up 'til now. Everybody did. Everybody still does. They say it over and over like they need to or else they might forget and actually talk some sense for a change. You all taught us to hate people we hardly know for no reason we could see. The funny thing is, when we were kids growing up, we played with them and nobody cared about who their Pa was. That all came later. Me and Serena, Abel, and Albert Lebrun and most all the small-fry on the mountain at the time, did. We wrestled and had us sword fights with sticks. King of the Hill, we played that and there was times when it got kinda rough and I come home with a black eye or a busted finger, but it weren't hateful. Let me tell you something, Ma. This is the last thing I got to say on the subject. When this is all over, I aim to marry Serena Barker. There, you heard it from me first."

Chapter Forty

Abel woke. He staggered through the front room and out the door. Five minutes later he reentered flailing his arms.

"Whooee, the hawk is out today. I like to froze to death out there. Morning, Jesse. Morning, Ma."

He pulled up a chair and inspected what was on a plate Addie had set out and covered with a cloth.

"Flapjacks. Well, that is something. What's the occasion?"

"It's Saturday, son. Today is Saturday."

"Yep, it is, sure enough. I thought we had the big breakfast on Sunday."

"One of us might not be here Sunday. Has you forgot?"

"One of us is...?"

"Ma, ain't nothing going to happen to me today. I told you. Don't pay her no mind, Abel, dive in. There's blackstrap molasses and some berries I picked off the vines on the fence."

"What did I forget?"

"Nothing. Eat up."

"Your brother is set to meet John Henry Lebrun noon today. One of them ain't going to be at the supper table tonight."

Abel's fork clattered to his plate and he turned pale. "Is it because of me, because I took that note and stood in your place?"

"No, Abel. You been away. It's the same thing as before only if you remember. He called me out right after the trial, right? It was put back a day or two. Finding you was more important than settling some old dare, right?"

"You're going to fight him today?"

"Not if I can help it."

"You ain't going to run, is you? Jesse, you can't run. They will call you a coward. You can't let them do that."

"Abel, you remember what we used to sing when we was kids? Sticks and stones can break my ones, but—"

"Names will never hurt me. Sure I do, but that was when we was little and the names were just mean things we said to rile each other. This ain't the same, Jesse. We got pride, we got—"

"Actually, the way I see it, it is pretty much the same. The only difference is, we don't settle up with a punch on the arm. And, also, if this is how we show our pride, Abel, we got nothing. Besides, ain't nobody going to die up on that mountain today. Not tomorrow either."

"But—"

"Hey, here's some news for you to chew on. Me and Serena is fixing to marry up. You can be the what-cha-call-it, groomsman."

"That sounds like a job at a stable. I ain't sure about that. You are? Marrying Serena? For real?"

"For real."

"Ma, did you hear that? Jesse is getting married. Wait, ain't she a Lebrun?"

"Abel, she is a Barker. You and me are Sutherlins. As far as this marriage is concerned, that is all. We are not McAdoos and they are not Lebruns. Period."

"But— "

"No buts. Now listen and listen close. I don't want either of you two up on the mountain when I do what I have to do. I am counting on nothing bad happening, but I can't control everybody up there. There will be a passel of folks from both sides and you know how easy it is for someone to do something stupid. So, just in case, you two hole up here."

"By Ned, if there's going to be a ruckus, I aim to be there, yes, sir.'

"No, you ain't Abel. You are still a mite yeasty from that whack you took on your head. The last place you need to be is in among some of the dumbest folk in the U.S. of A. Ma, you keep him here if you have to steal his britches."

"I am A plus, number-one fine and dandy, and hitting on all four, Jesse. You need me up there if them Lebruns—"

"No, Abel. You stay here and take care of Ma…just in case, okay?"

Abel did not look happy. Jesse guessed his mother would have her work cut out for her keeping him corralled. Jesse stood and pulled on his greatcoat.

"Where you going, son?"

"I have some loose ends to tie up, Ma. There are some people I need to talk to, some important types, some not so much. If this is going to work, the right folks has to be there and ready to keep an open mind and a shut mouth. I'll be back 'bout eleven. It's not even a mile to the top. That'll be plenty of time."

Jesse's intent was to have a talk with Big Tom. What happened later on the mountain could either lead to bloodshed or some sort of conversation. Which of these occurred would depend on what the heads of each clan said and did. Big Tom could make or break it.

He'd walked a quarter of a mile when Louise Knox rushed from her house and placed herself in his path.

"Morning, Weezy," he said.

"Where's he at? What have you done with my boy?"

"Pardon?"

"Sam ain't been home for two days. He didn't say anything to his Pa or me. Since you talked to him he ain't been the same."

"Weezy, as God is my witness, the last time I saw Sam he was chasing after that mule of yours across the pasture."

"You ain't seen him since?"

"Nope. He might be laying low on account of Little Tom being shot dead."

"Why would that have anything to do with my boy?"

"I told you once already, him, the two Crother boys, Little Tom, and cousin Anse were the ones who took it into their heads to string up Jake Barker the other night. Little Tom is dead. Maybe Sam thought whoever pulled that trigger that might not be done taking care of business."

"You did and I didn't believe you on account of the cuff you gave him. Sam really was mixed up that?"

"Gospel, Weezy."

"Oh my, and you think whoever was in on that devilment is in danger?"

"It's a guess, not a for sure. Things has got a little crazy around here lately, but if I was Sam, I'd be out of sight, too."

Louise Knox looked like she'd seen a ghost. She rushed back into her house screaming for her husband. Jesse waited a moment in case Uncle Bob appeared. He didn't. Jesse resumed his path toward Big Tom's but he couldn't let go of what Weezy said. If Sam has gone missing, what about the two Crother boys? Were they missing too? He veered off the path and headed toward Shaky Jim's

Jim Crother once held an important job down at the sawmill. That would be before R.G. took over. The previous owner, J. Owen Clanton, had a son and had assumed he would take over the mill when Clanton retired. The son, however, showed no interest in the lumber business. He'd gone over to Blacksburg to study business at VPI. There, he met up with some boys from Durham, North Carolina, and when he graduated followed them south. He joined a firm of stockbrokers, convinced his dad to invest in some shaky land deal out west somewhere. The long and short of it, the old man went bust, the boy went to jail, R.G. Anderson bought the mill at an auction, and Shaky elevated his habit of tapping a jug from now and again to now and now. He ended up unemployed. As a former professional man, he considered farming or any of the more menial pastimes beneath him. Nowadays he waited for opportunity to come knocking on his door. Times were hard at the Crother house.

Jesse knocked but nobody answered. While he considered pushing on in, he felt sure Jim was in there somewhere, probably asleep, the door cracked open an inch or two and his wife peeked around the jamb.

"How do, Miz Crothers. You remember me, Jesse Sutherlin? I was wondering if your boys were okay. Seems like Sam Knox had disappeared and since he and your two were tight, I wondered if maybe they were missing, too."

"Sure, I remember you. You went off to fight the damned Germans. Nope, I ain't got the foggiest idea where them two is from one day to the next. I am just sorry they missed out joining the Army like you done. Might have straightened them both out. If you want to know where they're at, and Sam can't say, you best be talking to that no-good cousin of yours."

"Anse?"

"Him." The door slammed shut. Jesse guessed Miz Crothers might have joined her husband in his new permanent occupation. So, the two boys were missing as well, or they weren't. Jesse wanted to warn them, but he couldn't do that if he couldn't find them. He could ask Anse, but the chances he'd get a straight answer from that quarter were pretty slim. He was headed to Big Tom's. He'd ask him about Anse and the other boys. They might all be missing if they thought Little Tom's murder was connected to the failed lynching. Big Tom, they said, knew everything about everybody. If he didn't have a line on them, nobody would.

Chapter Forty-one

The path to Big Tom's place looped around the Crothers' small holdings. Jesse decided he could save some time if he cut across their back acreage. The outbuildings were in pretty bad shape. No surprise there. The corn crib contained only a few rat-chewed cobs. The barn looked like it might fall apart in a heavy wind. Its siding looked like it hadn't seen a paintbrush since Appomattox. When buildings are abandoned by their owners, they seem to behave a lot like people. It's like they despair, or they've given up hope. All the evidence of a once tidy farm had fallen into shambles. The yard was covered in weeds and overgrowth. He didn't expect to see much in the vegetable patch, it being fall and near frost time. Sure enough, except for some onions gone to seed, the tract showed no sign that anyone had put a hoe or spade to it in years.

As he passed by the barn, he thought he heard voices. He stopped and listened. Sure enough, there were people in there. He strolled around the corner and forced open the building's only door. The track had rusted and the door screeched as he slid it sideways. Fortunately, he paused before stepping inside. The shotgun blast tore the air next to him.

"Hey, whoa, hold up there. Is that you two Crothers?"

"Who's asking?"

"It's me, Jesse. Why are you shooting? You come near to killing me."

"We heard you killed Little Tom just like you did Albert Lebrun."

"You heard what? I didn't kill anybody since I come home, least not yet and that includes them two. Why'd you think I shot Little Tom?"

"You was the one who found his body. There wasn't anybody else around. It musta been you."

"Whoever told you that is a liar. Look, if I had shot him, why would I have fired my gun in the air to get folks to come see? Wouldn't I have just sashayed on home and not said a word to anybody?"

"Maybe you is just plain stupid."

"Well, there's those who say so, but in this case, I wasn't. Listen to me, you two. There's something you blockheads need to be thinking hard on. If it weren't me that shot Little Tom, then there is somebody out there who did and is maybe not done shooting folks. Why would anyone want to do that to Little Tom, do you suppose? You mull on that for a spell. Then ask yourself, what do you two and Sam Knox have in common with Little Tom? You following me?"

"Maybe."

"Okay, here's another question. Where is Sam?"

"He lit out."

"Why?"

"Hell, we don't know. He said he stole his Ma's egg money and was headed to Roanoke where he was going to hop on a freight train west."

"He say why?"

"Nope."

"Might he have been the one who shot Little Tom?"

"Sam? Naw, he liked Tommy."

"Okay boys, a piece of advice, if you plan on hiding out in this building, keep your voices down. I heard you yakking ten yards away. Also, you might give a thought about finding yourself a better hiding place. You are easy targets in this old barn."

"How's that?"

"Well, if I wanted to kill you, all I'd have to do, is set this old falling down building on fire, which you all will admit wouldn't be much of a chore. Then, you'd either burn up or I'd shoot you when you come running out the door."

"Damn!"

"Yeah. When you rats do crawl out of your hole, one of you run over to the Knoxes' and tell them what you know about Sam. They are worried sick."

Jesse turned and set off again toward Big Tom's.

He found him sitting on his porch. He had his rifle barrel leaning up against one knee and was pulling an oily patch through it.

"Why are you here, Jesse? You're supposed to be getting ready to dispatch John Henry Lebrun."

Jesse glanced at the watch on his wrist. "Barely half past eight, Grandpa. I got plenty of time. I come to talk to you about that, though."

"What's to talk about? You get him or he gets you. Simple."

"Not really. You are heading up there with I don't know how many others. You know that the Lebruns will be there, too. I can't tell you to leave that Winchester behind, 'cause you won't, no matter what I say."

"You got that part right."

"You talked to Garland Lebrun, right?"

"I said I did. Did not enjoy the visit, but we did do some chin wagging."

"You said you believed him when he claimed that none of them had anything to do with Solomon's getting himself killed."

"I did. Like I said, he's a dying man and is thinking about the hereafter. Lying won't improve his chances of missing a trip to hell, which, in my mind ain't too good anyway, the son of a bitch."

"Here's what I think you should do. When you get up on the top, go find him and tell him that if he agrees to keep his guns with the safety on or strapped to the hip, you will, too."

"Why would I do anything so contrary?"

"Grandpa. This mountain is edgy. It won't take much to set off all kinds of trouble. One person shoots a gun, even if it's just showing off, and both sides will start firing. Before you know it, you all is dead and nothing is accomplished."

"And you think you can get something accomplished?"

"I hope to heaven I can. If not, I am dead. And if that happens, don't make me some kind of martyr, okay?"

"Some kind of what?"

"I'm saying, I ain't no saint. Nobody needs to die for me, is what I mean."

"You think Garland Lebrun will listen to me?"

"Like you said, he's a dying man and wants to get right with the Lord. I reckon he will."

"How'll I find him? You know everybody is going to be hunkered down in the trees."

"Well, sir, that is why I moved the meeting to the top of the Buffalo. There ain't enough trees up there to hide a litter of kittens much less the entire male portion of us and them. He'll be right out in the open or so far away it won't make no difference."

Jesse's next stop was the church. It would be called a "Primitive Baptist Church" by anyone given the task of making a record of the religious community later. The Reverend Parker B. Primrose was the preacher the congregation had raised up just last year. He and two others shared the pulpit most Sundays, but he was regarded as the head man because he could read and write a little, a very little. Preachers generally prided themselves on their complete absence of learning. A lack of any sign of education whatsoever ensured that the words that tumbled out of their mouths had to be God speaking. Because he read a little, Primrose was a rare and suspect exception. As preachers weren't paid, Primrose worked a patch of land back behind the church and he and his wife lived in a little house back beyond that. Jesse checked and found he wasn't in the church. Jesse walked to the cabin and knocked on his door. The wife opened it a crack, took one look at Jesse, and turned back into the house.

"You're the man who killed Albert Lebrun. You'll be wanting to talk to my husband, I imagine. Yes, indeed, time to get your sins spoke and see if there is any forgiveness out there for you, though how likely that'd be is a mystery to me."

"No, Ma'am. I ain't."

"You ain't what?"

"I ain't the man who stuck a knife in Albert. But you're right. I want to talk to your husband."

"Sin is sin. Lying about it makes it ten times worse, young man."

"Yessum, I know. The Reverend?"

"Through that door." She pointed to a door that for some reason had been painted purple. It wasn't a color you saw much on the mountain except in the wildflowers and they had this shade of purple beat to pieces. Primrose was a tiny man but they said he had the voice of a saint. Jesse conceded he was noisy, for sure. He had no idea what a saint sounded like but was pretty sure it wasn't like the Reverend. Primrose sat behind a table that served as a desk, but with the papers and jugs on it, had to weigh four times as much as he did. Even with the morning light on him, he barely cast a shadow.

"Reverend Primrose, it just come to me. Are you related to a Miss Primrose who works for Lawyer Bradford?"

"She is my sister who spent some time at schooling and who has joined the Methodists. Naturally, we ain't on speaking terms. How do you know her?"

"Lawyer Bradford and me are in business together, you could say. I met her in his office."

"You? You are in, did you say business, with Nicholas Bradford?"

"In a manner of speaking, yes."

"I reckon that can't lead to no good. The Devil is in the heads of them with too much book learning and the Bible is clear on lawyers and Pharisees being in cahoots with the Devil hisself. 'Then one of them, a lawyer, asked tempting him.' Matthew 22:35. 'None calleth for justice, nor pleadeth for truth: they trust in vanity, and speak lies; they conceive mischief, and bring forth iniquity,' Isaiah 59:4."

"You're leaving out, 'Owe no man anything, but to love one another: for he that loveth another hath fulfilled the law.' That'd be Paul taking to them Roman folk. This here is the twentieth century, Reverend. You need to get into it and just because we all talk and look like rubes, it don't mean we're all necessarily stupid. You know what they say, you can't tell a book by its cover."

"I got no truck with books."

"Pardon?"

"Reading is dangerous. You stick to the Good Book, maybe, but nowadays folks is reading them novels. They tell me there is women going plumb crazy with reading that trash."

"Okay. Well, I ain't here to discuss books. Here's what I come to see you about—"

"There is very little I can do about your sins, my boy. Murder is one the Lord will not set aside. 'Thou shalt not kill.' That's right in the Book."

"In France we killed a heap of German boys. Didn't nobody raise an eyelash about that killing. Some of you preachers even encouraged it."

"They were minions of the Devil. It were your duty to kill them. You was doing God's work."

"So, God has Himself a list of who is killable and who is not?"

"You don't need to get smart with me, young man. The Lord speaks to me and he says killing is a sin."

"It is. Don't He also say, 'If we confess our sins, he is faithful and just and will forgive us our sins and purify us from all unrighteousness.'? That'd be John the 'Postle. If I remember rightly it's in the same Book."

"I'm afraid…how do you come to know that?"

"I read at it from time to time. When you think you are likely to take a bullet any day like we did in the war, religion can get mighty comforting."

"Religion ain't about *comfort*, young man. If you be comfortable in the presence of the Lord, you ain't doing it right. Too many you young men with all that dancing and jazzing around… oh, I know a thing or two about that-ah. And thinking about the Bible is a dangerous thing-ah. Thinking is what sends you straight to hell-ah…"

"Preacher, I ain't here to talk about all that. That is your patch, but I reckon all that depends on which end of the Book you spend your time with. Now, to your question you seem like you answered for yourself already, I did not kill Albert, no matter what the local biddies are clucking. That's number one. Number two is, I want to get married as soon as possible."

"You have ruined a young woman and now you wish to—"

"Land sakes, for a preacher, you're sure quick to point a finger. Is that what they learned you in preacher school?"

"Well, I just reckoned that you all…"

"See, there you go again, jumping 'fore you look. I ain't got time for this. Next Saturday, here, getting married. Write that down."

Jesse slammed out.

"If it wasn't for Ma being so churched up, I swear I'd as soon go see the justice of the peace."

Chapter Forty-two

Time had started to catch up with Jesse. He slipped home and stuffed the things he'd need later in a poke and left before either his mother or brother could say anything. The last thing he wanted now was advice from either of them. What little time he had left, he wanted to spend someplace quiet. Like Garland Lebrun, Jesse needed to get right with the Almighty. Unlike Garland, he didn't really think he'd die, but he knew that he could have it wrong. One of the doctors he'd talked to in France, one who'd treated Solomon, said that soldiers were either fatalists or in a state of denial. They either believed with certainty they were going to die or they were never going to, not right away, anyway. A few, he'd said, bounced back and forth between the two beliefs like an India rubber ball. Jesse wasn't sure he had the first part pegged. But he understood it generally. Men in the trenches all thought they were going to die. He guessed that's what the doctor meant. There were days when he shared that feeling. A lot of days. Then there were the times, like when he fell in the German trench, when he knew he wasn't. That would be denial, right? Now he wasn't so sure. Was he in that denial state? Was he fooling himself? Maybe. So, just to be sure, spend some time thinking about the hereafter.

He wandered over to The Oaks and sat on the steps of the Spring House. His property, if he lived through the day. His and Serena's. Property ownership had never featured highly in his thinking before now. Land passed from father to son, sometimes to daughters. If there were more than one son and both wanted to stay on it, it would be halved or quartered. After a while, the plots weren't large enough to sustain a family and the people would move on. A hundred years ago, there was land aplenty and for the taking out west in places like Illinois and out on the plains. Even as late as 1889 you could have joined the land rush out in Oklahoma. But things were different now. Land, if you wanted it, had a price and that price kept going up. People said, "God ain't making no more land." It was all mostly taken. And here he was sitting on a little under twelve acres of land in a place where folks had crowded themselves into tiny little played-out farms. This would be considered luxury by mountain standards and he owned it.

He heard a footstep.

"I thought I might find you here," Serena said, and plopped down beside him.

"You shouldn't have come," he said. He thought a minute and added, "But, I'm glad you did."

She smiled. It was one of those secret smiles that women make when there is something on their mind that they are cherishing, but aren't talking about. They pop up a lot early in courtship. You don't see them as often later and that's a pity.

"What?"

"I was remembering, that's all."

"Listen, about last night—"

"Don't you dare, Jesse."

"Don't I dare to what?"

"Last night was the most wonderfulest night of my life. Don't you go ruining it with thinking you need to apologize for spoiling me. You didn't. We came together, the both of us, and I don't believe I will ever feel that way again. I don't want that memory ruined by morning male guilty talk."

"Oh."

"How many women get to find what we did under the stars?"

"Not many, I reckon."

They sat silent for a while. Jesse tried to put himself in Serena's mind and discover what it was she was feeling. He felt pretty darn good, but he guessed that Serena was at a different place, thinking about what they did up on the mountain.

"This is a nice patch, don't you think?"

"I know you think so, Jesse."

"You don't?"

"It's fine."

"But...?"

"It's here on the mountain, Jesse. I don't want to die on the mountain. I don't care how nice this place is, it's still smack dab in the middle of Buffalo Mountain."

"Building a little house here don't appeal, I understand. But the foundation of the old place is in really good order. It wouldn't be any trouble putting up a house on part of it. We could... wait, hear me out...We could settle here for a spell. Just long enough to get some money and then move on. Shoot, we don't even know where we want to land. So, we set up camp, you could say, and then we'd have a place to launch from."

"I know that sounds sensible and all. I just worry, Jesse. See, people are a little like trees. If you make yourself comfortable in a place too long, you put down roots. Every year that goes by, the roots grow deeper into the ground. Then one day, you wake up and discover you're stuck. The roots is so deep, you can't move. You can never move. Like I said, I do not want to spend all my days on this mountain."

"Not even with me?"

"Don't do that, Jesse. Don't make it an either/or. That isn't fair."

"No, it's not." He stripped the bark of a twig and stuck it in his mouth to chew. "I promise you this one thing, Serena. I will never tie you down. I will never ignore what your heart says it needs."

She leaned her head on his shoulder. He put his arm around her and cupped her breast. She didn't mind that at all.

"Time is running out, Jess. You got to go."

"I do."

Neither moved.

"Jess, I'm scared."

"Don't be. I am a survivor. I been in worse places with worser odds and done alright. You won't be a widow before you are a bride, I promise."

"Jess, I love you, you know that, but sometimes I think you have butterflies instead of a brain. You can't know what the future is going to bring."

"No, you got that right. It's just, I can't believe that God would get us this far and then pull the roof down over our heads. It just don't make sense."

"You have a lot more trust in the Almighty than me, then."

"That's okay. I am happy to believe for the both of us." He stood and picked up his sack. It clanked when he slung it over his shoulder. "I don't want you to come up there, Serena."

"Why ever not?"

"Who knows how this is going to end. People are itching to start a brawl. If that happens, most likely the folks not in on it are the ones to get hurt."

"That's not the reason and you know it. In spite of what you say, you're afraid it might turn out bad for you and you don't want me to be there to see it."

"Serena—"

"What did you say last night? You said we are married except for saying the words in front of a preacher. Well, I believe that. So no, we haven't said the words yet, but we took them into our hearts, didn't we? And if I remember them right from Edward and Sally's wedding, they say you and me have 'become one flesh.' Well, that's a certain fact. They also say, 'for better or for worse, in sickness and in health, 'til death us do part.' Well, if you believe all that, then I have to be with you even if we get the worse and the death part 'fore we get the good things. I'm coming, Jesse, and that's that."

Chapter Forty-three

Jesse and Serena started up the slope toward the summit. They were alone. Everyone else either made a decision to stay home and lay low or climbed to the top using one of the two major pathways. One snaked up the east side and wasn't quite as easy a climb as the more direct one on the west face. She held Jesse's hand and even though it made climbing over fallen trees and rocks more difficult, he didn't let go. He should have been calculating his strategy for the fight ahead, but that no longer held his attention. What would be, would be, and there's an end to that. Instead, his thoughts were on the two of them and what they'd done, what they'd promised each other, what could be. Serena seemed to be having a great deal of difficulty keeping a serious expression on her face. What a way to start a life together.

"You know most everybody, all the men, at least, are going to be up there on that meadow. The very same one we married up on, in a way."

"I know that, Jesse. Seems kind of crazy appropriate, in a way."

"I don't see how."

She giggled. "Well, we already spilled a little blood up there. Maybe the meadow fairies will figure that's enough and we'll all shake hands and go home and have a nice supper."

"You...I didn't..."

"It's the way we're put together, Jesse. Most natural thing in the world. I got to admit, I am a tiny bit sore down there, though. It's a good sore."

"I would say I'm sorry, but I ain't."

"Me neither."

They paused a moment to check on their progress.

"I met this Scotsman over in France. Did you know they went fighting wearing little dresses?"

"They what? They wear dresses? In the fighting? You are joking me."

"Little ones, short. They have a funny name for them, but I can't recall what it is. Gospel truth. The soldiers called themselves the Black Watch. Don't that sound wicked? And they have this thing they blow in to make music. It has pipes sticking out the one side and a little whistle thing in front. Makes a helluva racket. They stand up and play on that thing and march straight at the enemy guns. Damnedest thing I ever heard. The Germans we took prisoner I told you about, they said they were more afraid of them Black Watch Scotchmen that anything they had to deal with."

"Well, that is plain strange."

"War is strange. Anyways, I was talking to him and he said when he was to home they all would meet one time a year at a thing they called the Gathering of the Clans. All the different families would get together from all over and play games, dance, and eat."

"And?"

"And I think when we get to the top, that is pretty much what we are going to see today, the Gathering of the Clans, only we ain't going to play games, dance, or eat."

"Wouldn't it be nice if we were?"

"It would, though watching Big Tom or Garland Lebrun dance might not be much of a treat."

• • ● • •

People were still arriving when they reached the summit. No one said anything to them, although, a few gave them a look or two. Serena just smiled.

"Now then, Jesse Sutherlin, where should I put myself? Am I a Lebrun and should I stand over on the east or am I now one of you all and should stand on the west?"

"I reckon, right here up top and sort of in the middle."

She waved to her brother. "Jake, come on over here with me."

Jake hesitated, looked around and shuffled over.

"How do, Jake," Jesse said. "I need to give you a warning. You did one for me, so here's the come-back. It could get a little uneasy here in a minute or two. If I manage to get off killing John Henry, we have a go at finding us a murderer. That could be trouble for you 'cause you might get a mention."

"Why would my name be brought up?"

"Serena told me about your midnight occupation, for one."

"She didn't."

"I did. Jake, you could get yourself killed."

"Yeah, well..."

"Them boys who were helping you—"

"What boys? I don't know what you are talking about, Jesse."

"As I was about to say, Anse and them will give you up in a heartbeat to save their own necks. If I remember correctly, they already done it once."

"What are you saying, Jess?" Serena said. Her smile had disappeared.

"I'll let Jake tell you. Just that with Little Tom in his grave, what he and some others worked out about the McAdoo stills and where they were, could come back to bite him. Jake, if you need a head start off the mountain, now would be a good time to take it. I have a meeting to go to. Serena, be ready to scatter, just in case trouble heads this way."

"Why would—?"

"Just keep alert and don't think you have to be brave or something."

Jesse turned and made his way down the slope toward the flat area he'd picked for his meeting with John Henry. He shook his head in frustration. Two steps forward one step back or was it one step forward and two back? Serena would be okay with what he had to do, wouldn't she?

The hillsides were filling up with men, mostly, although a few women, his mother included, stood uncomfortably in the background. Abel tried to hide behind Uncle Bob Knox, but Jesse saw him. The meadow buzzed like a hive of bees in a full blooming flower garden. Some folks muttered threats, others encouragement to one or the other of the combatants. He tried to ignore them all. He veered off to talk to Big Tom.

"You able to talk to Garland?"

"I did. He said he'd try to keep his folk calm. Me too, but it ain't easy."

"If they just keep them shooting irons pointed down or stuck in their belts, it'll have to do. Where's Anse?"

"I got him in tow.""

"Good. Don't let that hothead shoot off his mouth and blow this up into a all out war."

John Henry had his knife out and was showing off to the delight of the Lebrun men. He'd a trick he did with his knife. He'd flip it up in the air and it would spin and drop back into the palm of his hand, handle first. The sun glittered off the blade as he flipped higher, two, three, four rotations and, plop, it would land in his hand. It looked dangerous. If the knife were half as sharp as Jesse's, it was. He grinned at Jesse.

"You ready, Jesse Sutherlin? Are you ready to get your guts spilled?"

"Big talk there, John Henry. Give me a minute."

Jesse walked a step or two to his right to stand next to a stunted tree, no taller or bigger around than a sapling, an old and gnarled survivor of the altitude and wind that gusted constantly across this part of the mountain. Jesse dropped his sack and removed his knife. He slipped it from its sheath. John Henry increased the height of his tosses. Jesse pulled a sheet of paper from his pocket, unfolded it and held it in his left hand. It fluttered in the wind and each time it hit the knife blade, a strip sheared off.

"Judas Priest," he heard a voice behind him say. "That sumbitch is sharp."

John Henry's expression shifted from taunting to serious. He missed the timing on his knife flipping routine and had to jerk his hand back at the last second or he might have lost a finger or two. Jesse reached into his sack again and pulled out his entrenching tool.

"Well, what the hell is that? I guess you came prepared, Jesse," John Henry said. "Are you planning on digging your grave before I carve you up or have you given that job to Big Tom to do after?"

Jesse clipped the lower limbs from the tree next to him and pointed at the trunk with the digging end of the tool.

"John Henry, would you say your wrist on the arm holding your knife is about this thick?"

"What, my wrist? Maybe, sure, a little thicker I think."

"Here, then?" Jesse nicked the bark to mark the spot.

"Okay, so what?"

Jesse swung the small shovel up across his body. He gripped the handle at its end in his right hand. The spade end he held in his palm just short of the metal. He stared at John Henry for what seemed like a minute. Then he twisted his body to his right, slid his left hand down so that he grasped the handle at its end with both hands. He looped his arms over his head, the shovel pointed skyward and Jesse twisted his whole body around. The shovel sailed in an arc, down and around. It sliced through the tree trunk, where he'd marked it, like a hot knife through butter. The tree lifted up and over and its cut end landed at John Henry's feet.

"Now then, John Henry, you got a decision to make. See, there is a murderer standing on this hill. He's killed two of my cousins and one of yours. If we don't work this out together, he'll kill some more. He's pretty much got to. So, do we talk about that, or do I use this entrenching tool to lop off your arm or maybe separate your head from your shoulders?

Chapter Forty-four

No one said a word. John Henry tried to swallow and failed. Jesse lowered his entrenching tool and let the spade end rest on the grass. The handle he held loosely in his hand. No one doubted he could bring it up swinging in an instant. The crowd closed in to form a tighter circle around them.

John Henry finally managed to clear his throat. "You can't do nothing to me, Jesse Sutherlin. You just try."

"Shut up, John Henry," said Garland Lebrun. "If he wanted to, he could have chopped you to pieces. He didn't. He showed you he could and gave you a choice. He didn't have to do that. Now, I ain't about to lose another young'un over this." He turned to Jesse. "Tell us what you want, but first, tell me where'd you learn to use that shovel like that?"

"Mister Lebrun, war is a messy business and you never know what you need to do 'til you're smack dab in the middle of it. In training, they taught us to use our bayonets when we come to hand-to-hand fighting. But the fact is, it's way too crowded in a trench to do anything that's stuck on the end of a rifle. When they jumped into one of ours or we jumped into theirs, we'd squeeze off a round. Drop the damn rifle and grab anything handy that you could swing in a tight place. Knives mostly. The Germans were the ones who first put an edge on an entrenching tool. Hell, we all had them slung on our backs anyway, so we done the same. You can see the damage they can do."

"I can. What do you want from us?"

"Here's what I got." Jesse raised his voice so that everyone could hear him. "Anybody knows more, jump on in. My cousin Solomon was shot in the back last week. Naturally all us McAdoos assumed it were one of you Lebruns that did it."

"Not all of us, Garland. Jesse didn't." Big Tom stood across from Garland Lebrun. He didn't look happy, but then, nobody did except maybe Serena and she'd the good sense to stay out of sight.

"You didn't?"

"It wasn't that I didn't. It was I didn't want to act unless we had some proof it was. That's all. Okay, I walked the scene where Solomon was shot. I think someone saw what happened that day, but they're too scared to say anything. I think if I can find that person, or them people—I believe there was two of them, I might know the who of it."

"And you think we can help you do that?"

"Yes, sir."

"How?"

"If you and Big Tom will, ask all the small boys standing around here to shuck off their shoes and walk across this muddy stream bank."

"Why the hell for?"

"Trust me, just do it, please. Abel, I know you're around here somewhere. Come on over here and help me out. If we have two lines, it'll go faster. You know what we're looking for?'

Abel separated himself from the crowd. He looked much better. The excitement seemed to be the right medicine for him. "A crookedy toe?"

"Right. Okay start them coming."

Any hesitation on the boys' part melted from the looks to two old men gave them. They marched across the mud muttering under their breath about how they like to froze their feet off. A dozen had made it across when Abel shouted. "I got 'em." He had Levi Eveleth by the collar. "I'd recognize that footprint anywhere."

Jesse walked over and checked. "Okay, you all, you can put your shoes back on. Levi Eveleth, tell me who was with you at Big Tom's still when Solomon got shot?"

"Weren't nobody."

"It was your brother, Eli, wasn't it?"

"Answer the man, son," Garland said, not kindly.

"Yeah, it was him."

"Eli, over here."

The boy, who couldn't have been more than nine, his feet almost coming out of still untied shoes which had to be two sizes too big, clomped over to them.

Jesse tried not to look as mean as Garland Lebrun and Big Tom McAdoo. "You boys tell me what you saw."

The two looked at each other.

"Didn't see nothing."

"That won't do. See you left footprints at the scene. You, Levi, has got a funny toe. That's how I know it was you."

"Tell Sutherlin what you know." Garland Lebrun was in no mood to waste time. He had a reason not to.

"Yes, sir." The two boys looked at each other and at Garland Lebrun. "We saw Solomon McAdoo heading off into the woods and were fixing to sneak up on him and shoot off Eli's squirrel gun, you know, to make him go all shaky, but we didn't get a chance."

"You didn't. Why?"

"We come to the edge of the clearing like and by golly damn there were a still there. We didn't know whose it was. So we stopped dead. I mean if we was caught in someone's place like that we could have been shot our own selves. But old Solomon didn't have no gun so, we figured we might could and we was standing back a little waiting for our chance."

"Chance? You were bent on tormenting him?"

"Well, yes sir, we was, but then this other man come into the clearing holding a big scatter gun like maybe he had the same idea."

"What man? Who did you see?" Big Tom nearly shouted.

"Don't know. He had this big bandanna round his face like a bank robber or something."

"You didn't see his face? Hair color?"

"He had on a hat, but darkish like him, not yellow hair like you-all's"

"Okay the man came into the clearing. Then what?"

"Well, he started to sneak up on Solomon, like I said. You know, to make him go all crazy-like. He had that gun pointed up in the air and his finger must have been on the trigger 'cause he tripped, maybe on a root or something, and lost his balance and he sort of staggered, and the gun went off –Blam! It like to take off Solomon's head, it did."

"It was an accident?" Big Tom asked.

"Yes sir, Mister McAdoo. That is surely what it appeared to be."

Jesse shook his head. "You could say so. I'm thinking who-ever did that had no business tormenting Solomon. That part was deliberate. Solomon deserved something better than the disrespect he got from you all. It were a meanness that cost a good man his life. So, you call it what you want. I'm saying it's murder one way or 'tother and has led to two other killings, Little Tom and Albert. Okay, you two, git."

The boys scuttled off, glad to be free of the adults and the angry looks they were getting from both sides of the meadow.

Big Tom shook his head. "So, you're saying Solomon is dead because some knucklehead wanted to torment him. A stupid accident. What about Little Tom? Are you saying the same man killed him? How you going to hook them two up?"

"I do say that. The person who done him in is the same. See, I think Little Tom was on his way to see you, Grandpa, and 'fess up about Albert Lebrun's killing and got waylaid."

Garland Lebrun stepped up and faced Jesse. "Albert? You think you can tie Albert's killing to the same person, too?"

"In a big, fat bow, yes sir, Mister Lebrun."

"I'd like to hear how."

"I reckon we all would, Jesse."

"Remember I said in court that I saw three men follow Albert after he left me. The blockhead we got for a sheriff didn't want to hear that, of course. He has an itch to put me and some others of us standing around here in jail for…well, never you mind what. It were a long time ago and we ain't here to ponder on his marriage problems and his wife's shenanigans. Just say we need to keep a sharp eye out for that Jasper in the future, boys."

A few of the younger men standing in the crowd snorted or shouted "Woo-hee."

"Anyway, about them three that took off after Albert. I believe Little Tom and Sam Knox were two of them who I saw follow Albert after we had our talk. The third one is who stabbed Albert."

"Who was it?"

"Not yet, Grandpa. It's like who shot Solomon. You all were ready to shoot one of the Lebruns on a maybe. I got the same problem. Thinking I know and proving it out are two different things. You all need proof, right?"

"If it were any one of us, I sure do. I reckon Lebrun, here, does, too."

Garland Lebrun shifted his chew, right cheek to left, and spit. "I'm listening."

"Okay, then. We'll talk about Albert and then Little Tom. I need to borrow John Henry for a minute. John Henry, if you wanted to knife me, not in a fight where we are squared off at each other like just now, but just kill me, how'd you go about it? Come at me like you would."

Lebrun raised his fist as if it held a knife, head high, and stepped forward. He brought his fist down on Jesse's chest—a little harder than necessary, Jesse thought.

"Okay, you seen what he done. See, that won't work. Albert took the same training in the Army as me. John Henry, do that again. You all watch." John Henry repeated the approach and found himself on the ground with his arm nearly twisted out of its socket. "See, Albert would have known how to do that. Whoever stabbed Albert must have known or guessed that and he'd do something different. John Henry, if you wanted to kill someone with no fuss, what'd you do?"

"I'd come up behind and throw an arm around his throat like this and stab him in the chest right here."

"Right. Now look where your knife went in. It's about in the middle of my chest. You would have got me in the heart, ain't that right?"

"Yeah. Albert was stabbed there."

"He was, but the coroner said what killed him was a deep stab wound behind his left collarbone. Could you do that holding me like you are?"

John Henry looked at his arm and knife hand and shook his head.

"You can't because your elbow is in the way."

"How then?"

"Suppose you were left-handed."

John Henry pulled his left arm from around Jesse's throat and wrapped his right instead. "Then I could."

"Grandpa, do you recall the story of Ehud? It's in the Book, in Judges someplace."

"The feller that stabbed King Whosis, Eglon. The guards didn't notice his sword 'cause it were on the wrong side of his outfit."

"That's the one."

Big Tom combed his beard with his fingers. "The son of a bitch who killed Albert is a left-handed man?"

"He certainly used his left hand, yep. It's the only way Albert gets stabbed the way it got done. How about everybody who's left-handed put them up."

A half dozen men raised their hands.

"You're saying one of them did it?"

"Anse, you ain't raised your hand."

"What are you getting at? Everybody knows I'm right-handed."

"But not lately, ain't that so? You got a broke wrist I gave you when you tried coming at me like John Henry just did, knife high. If you tried using that busted right hand to stick somebody, it'd hurt, I expect. Certainly wouldn't go in very deep."

"No, you don't Jesse. You ain't gonna get me this time. Grandpa, he's making this all up. Everybody knows he done it. Ain't that right? Jesse Sutherlin killed Albert Lebrun. If it weren't for that flatlander judge being all soft on war heroes, he'd be swinging by now. We can fix that. He should be strung up this very minute."

"You'd best keep your mouth shut, son," Garland said and spit again, this time barely missing Anse's boot.

"Grandpa, here's how it was. Anse, Sam Knox, and Little Tom followed me that night. I ain't sure why, but I'm thinking they were still smarting from when I run them off the night they tried to lynch Jake Barker. Maybe they thought they could get even for what I done, I don't know. Whatever, they happened to be in the woods when Albert showed up and heard us talking. It was them three that followed Albert. Now, Anse knew if Albert were to help me, we would have got around to him a lot quicker. Killing Albert ended that and also threw a monkey wrench in everything else. But just to make sure, you remember it was Anse who first swore to Sheriff Franklin that I was the one who found Solomon and then, as the sheriff's favorite ass-kiss, also swore I was the last to see Albert alive. Since no one on the mountain, especially a Lebrun, would ever have called in the sheriff for a killing, I'm guessing it were Anse that did that too. He figured the sheriff would be happy to lock me up and maybe find enough to get me hung after all."

"You watch it, Jesse. You better be careful how you talk. I ain't nobody's—"

Big Tom collared Anse. "Shut up, boy. I'll tell you when to speak."

"Okay, so, when that didn't work, he tried to ambush me out on the bluff. Trouble was, Abel showed up wearing my old Army jacket, not me, and Anse mistook him for me and Abel ended up being the one stabbed and hit on the head. You with me so far?

Big Tom rocked back on his heels and studied Jesse and then Anse in turn. "Go on."

"Right. Now right here I am guessing because I can't ask him, but it appears that killing Albert was too much for Little Tom or maybe the ambush by the creek that dropped Abel was it, I ain't sure. It was one thing when they like to lynch Jake Barker, but killing Albert for no reason except Anse said they should? No. Little Tom drew himself a line in the dirt, you could say."

Jesse caught Frank McAdoo's eye. "He reckoned what he'd done weren't right and let on he was aiming to tell you everything. Anse couldn't have that so he met him out by Big Tom's place. I expect he had that little derringer Big Tom gave him in his left-hand pocket. They argued and Anse shot Little Tom once straight through the pocket, then he jerked the pistol out and shot him in the head. San Knox figured this all out and took off before Anse did him, too."

"He's a liar. He's just covering up for hisself. He was the one who only *said* he found Little Tom dead but he coulda killed him and that ain't all. Ever since the night we...You ask Jake Barker. He knows all about your still and where it's at. He's a poacher and Solomon must have caught him in the act. Well, there you go and—"

Big Tom froze Anse with a look. "Shut your mouth, boy."

"Solomon didn't have a gun, Grandpa. You know that. Jake might or might not have been what Anse says, but if he were, no way would he have been shot by Solomon." Jesse wheeled on Anse. "And I am 'bout up to here with you, cousin. Now, you show Grandpa your left coat pocket."

"That ain't nothing. It's just a tear I got on a briar bush."

"Grandpa, does that look like maybe a bullet made that hole?"

"Damn you to hell, Anse McAdoo, what have you done?"

Anse had his mouth open and seemed busy thinking up an answer, but he never got past, "Honest, it wasn't me. It were accidental like and I didn't...Little Tom, see, he—"

"You killed my son!" Frank McAdoo yelled.

Heads turned toward Frank. In that frozen moment, a gun went off from somewhere in the crowd. A blood stain bloomed on Anse's shirtfront. He dropped to the ground, coughed up some blood and lay still.

In the silence that followed, Big Tom pushed Anse's corpse with his toe, turned toward the crowd, and cocked his head toward the paths leading away down the mountain.

"We're done here. Everybody, go home."

Chapter Forty-five

Men started to shuffle off. A few stood still, as if they weren't quite sure whether Big Tom's declaration that there was no more to be done was either true or wise. Big Tom motioned to four of them to collect Anse McAdoo. He needed to be carried off the top and taken home to be given a proper burial.

"Not so fast." A tallish man, obviously not from the mountain, pushed his way into their midst. He had on what might be considered a shabby outfit anywhere except on the mountain. His tweed newsboy's hat didn't match his coat, and his trousers sagged at the knee, but by mountain standards, he could have been a store window manikin. He flipped his tweed jacket back and flashed a badge. The hammers of a dozen rifles snicked back. He may or may not have heard that. If he did, he didn't flinch. "I am Lieutenant Quentin D. Thompson of the Virginia State Police. This man was murdered in cold blood right here and now and I aim to take in whoever did it." The rustle of pistols being drawn followed.

"We settle our own affairs, Mister Policeman. If you have any sense in that brain box of yourn, you'll turn yourself around and skedaddle as fast as them fancy citified shoes will take you."

"I might, and I might not." He yanked a whistle from his coat pocket and blew it. Seven uniformed troopers loomed up over the crest of the mountain and started down the slope.

"Whoever shot this man, step forward and we won't have any trouble."

Six McAdoos and four Lebruns took a step toward him.

"What is it with you people? You go in for murder like normal people eat peanuts."

"This here weren't no murder. You all from the bottomland don't have no place here. We found this man guilty of killing one of our own and the score is settled. That's it, mountain justice. Now, tell them fellers in those monkey suits to git on back where they come from."

"If you all won't tell me who did this, I'll have to go about it differently. One of you has a recently fired gun. My men will check every one of them and when we find it, we'll have our man."

Two dozen men raise their weapons skyward and fired.

Quentin Thompson pivoted on his heel in a complete circle. He saw the expressions on the faces of more mountain men than he cared to contemplate having to tussle with. He blew two short blasts on his whistle. The uniforms stopped, turned and moved off.

"One of these days, you yokels will join civilization. I will probably be collecting my pension by then." He took a step toward Jesse and fished a business card from his vest pocket. "Lawyer Bradford was right. You are the exception to the rule. I listened to you just now, son. I was impressed. You have grit, common sense, and a logical mind. If you ever want to do police work, you look me up."

Quentin D. Thompson took his men off the mountain and never came back.

Serena and Jake waved to Jesse as he worked his way through the crowd. She practically danced up to him.

"Oh, Jess, you were wonderful."

Jesse put his arm around her and smiled. Whether from delight at seeing her or relief for still being alive it'd be hard to say. Jake inspected his shoes and then looked up.

"Thank you, Jesse, for keeping me out of this. Besides the hooch poaching, or maybe because of it, I know you could have made a case for me being the one who shot Little Tom and scared off Sam Knox. I'd be lying if I said I didn't consider doing it after they near to hanged me, believe you me. If it hadn't been for Serena, I damn well would have, but we lost our Ma and Pa and risking one more death might have done her in. I appreciate what you done. I do."

Serena put her hand on his shoulder. "I ain't no wilting flower, Jake. Going after them five morons would have been stupid, but I'd have understood."

Jesse gave her a squeeze. "Tell you the truth, Jake, you were one of my choices for a bit. That didn't please me none but the pointers was all in your direction there. But I couldn't shake the notion that it seemed likely the killings were all connected. If that was so, then Albert's death meant it probably wasn't you. True, with him in the picture it would have been tough, but he's a Lebrun and so are you. He wouldn't have turned you out. So, then it all came down to figuring out who else had a reason and that lead me to Anse McAdoo. He witnessed against me and he was so hot to run this into a full out war, I had to wonder. Why was he so danged hot to do that? Then I got to thinking about dogs chasing their tails and it occurred to me that maybe a feud between us all was a good way to hide a murder. Solomon had his head about blown off. That didn't look like no ordinary murder, so what was it? Then I remembered those boys tormenting Solomon, and Anse being one of the chief ones who did it and it started to come together. Man and boy, he has been courting a bullet in the brain all his life. I don't know what happened that made him so confounded ornery, but he always was. Maybe his Ma dropped him on his head when he was little. Anyway, you were clear except for the moonshine poaching. You need to get yourself out of that business, Jake, or somebody, someday is going to send you to the place where you'll need to get you some asbestos underwear."

"I'll see you Monday at the sawmill, if you think there is a chance for work there."

Serena turned to her brother. "And you might be getting yourself ready to be moving in with Edward and Sally soon.

Jesse's house has too many people and too few rooms and we will need our privacy."

"You want me to move out? Wait a minute. Why am I moving?"

"Me and Jesse are getting married and need to be together. Don't fret. It'll only be 'til we get us a little house built on our land."

To receive a free catalog of Poisoned Pen Press titles, please provide your name, address, and e-mail address in one of the following ways:

Phone: 1-800-421-3976
Facsimile: 1-480-949-1707
Email: info@poisonedpenpress.com
Website: www.poisonedpenpress.com

Poisoned Pen Press
6962 E. First Ave. Ste 103
Scottsdale, AZ 85251

CPSIA information can be obtained
at www.ICGtesting.com
Printed in the USA
BVOW03s1435090117
473010BV00001B/7/P